The Peace Terrorist

THE
Peace
Terrorist

STORIES BY
CAROL MASTERS

*For Zoltan &
Debi — Thanks
for your commitment
& grace !*

Carol Masters

Minnesota Voices Project Number 64

NEW RIVERS PRESS 1993

Cover art by Paul Chillman
Paul Chillman was born in Minneapolis in 1971. He studied holography
and computer graphic design at the School of the Art Institute of Chicago,
and received his B.F.A. in 1993.

The publication of *The Peace Terrorist* has been made possible by
generous grants from the Dayton Hudson Foundation on behalf of
Dayton's and Target Stores, the Jerome Foundation, the Metropolitan
Regional Arts Council (from an appropriation by the Minnesota Legisla-
ture), the North Dakota Council on the Arts, the South Dakota Arts
Council, and the James R. Thorpe Foundation.

Additional support has been provided by the General Mills Foundation,
Land o' Lakes, Inc., Liberty State Bank, the McKnight Foundation, the
Star Tribune/Cowles Media Company, the Tennant Company Founda-
tion, and the contributing members of New Rivers Press. New Rivers
Press is a member agency of United Arts.

New Rivers Press books are distributed by

The Talman Company
131 Spring Street, Suite 201 E-N
New York NY 10012

The Peace Terrorist has been manufactured in the United States of
America for New Rivers Press, 420 N. 5th Street/Suite 910, Minneapolis,
MN 55401. First Edition.

*For my loves, especially Ken, Paul, Carl
& Kerri, my mother Katy, and the peace movement.
Special thanks to the beloved communities
Onionskin writers; St. Andrews Lutheran Church,
Minneapolis; Women Against Military Madness.*

*"We are not yet what we shall be
but we are growing toward it.
The process is not yet finished
but it is going on.
This is not the end
but it is the road.
All does not yet gleam in glory
but all is being purified."*

—Martin Luther

Acknowledgements

"In the General Population, in Ordinary Time" appeared in excerpt in *The Origin of Tigers*, an anthology of selections by winners of the 1990 Loft-McKnight awards, Minneapolis, 1990.

"Bottom of the Sea" is forthcoming in *Grounds for Peace*, published by Women Against Military Madness and Women Poets of the Twin Cities, Minneapolis, 1993.

Contents

The Bottom of the Sea

DECEMBER 11, 1985

Myra the bag lady is at the downtown library today. Hunched over the sun's weak glints off the library table, she blows on the coals of her hands. I am glad to see her. She affirms my existence as a free person, out on the streets for the first time in thirty days. My husband said once I'd probably end up as a bag lady; I don't know if it was a threat or a warning, so I study her covertly.

I am doubly free today. Not only am I on work release from the Huber Correctional Facility, released to Hand-Kenyon, Inc., my employer, but Debbie my boss has assigned me to research law firms at the library. My spirit dances in its chains, incognito prisoner of the state and of the usual workplace boredom. My double balls-and-chains are invisible to the librarians and the clientele, I'm sure.

I have to return in a few hours, queue up for the workhouse transport at 4th and 4th, behind the old Minneapolis courthouse where the bearded Mississippi, Father of Waters, lounges, ample male flesh naked in chilly marble. Too bad. My mostly male criminal cohort are a smokier lot, puffing away on the back of the bus, where smoking is illegal. Our conveyance is an old school bus, Medicine Lake Lines, as in, take your medicine — which amuses me. Middle class, at least working, criminals carted to and fro to be reschooled in social usefulness.

Still, I feel free. The impermanence of my position, breathing the unwalled though tired, polluted air of downtown, enchants me. On the way to the library, I'm smug, watching the fatigued shoppers, the hurried secretaries and clerks jostle each other near City Center. I have nothing better to do than watch them, carrying Huber walls with me like protection. I'm an alien, practicing mental kindliness for a few unmonitored hours. I meet more eyes than I'm used to meeting on the streets, and make my requests of the reference gentlepeople with an assured smile. Hey, I'm here for the long haul, I can't leave, my eyes say.

Not that Myra will meet my eyes. She won't recognize me, anyway; I remember her only because I worked at Saint Stephen's shelter two or three nights. Saint Stephen's wore me down. I couldn't sleep there, even though the volunteers' mats were removed from the rows of homeless sleepers, and were tucked away in the telephone room. The walls were ineffective sound barriers. I heard every crackle and creak of the plastic mats, every grunt and sigh of the sleepers. My chest ached, maybe from trying to hold still, most of the night.

Myra is a recognizable character in Minneapolis. Her crow-black hair is spray trained to close over her white face like shutters. Even with her head down, the hair swings to reveal high red makeup on her cheeks and lips, like embers of a banked fire. Her fleshy hips and buttocks roll in a firm and energetic stride: in black boots, black on black skirt, black jersey, two black sweaters, she is inexorable as earth, moving like a mud slide, pedestrians parting to avoid being carried along. Myra takes care of herself.

Today her padded (black) jacket is folded to a neat square on the chair beside her. She's as alone at the long library table as she is at the shelter, where the guys give her lots of room, including clotheslines hung with blankets between her mat and the next ones. My first night at the shelter, I thought the privacy was granted because she was older and was one of the few women — this was 1984, before the influx of women and children into the shelters in Minneapolis and St. Paul. Then I overheard someone say she spits if you get too close.

Today, I have the nerve to draw closer to her independent fire — kind of an outlaw camp, I think. We share an instinct for survival, and I want her to know it. My eyes, red as any scholar's, attest to the tempering of thirty days of adversity and forebearance. Actually they're red from the smoke on the cellblock and the back of the bus. I sit at the next table, facing hers, and ignore her quick scowl.

The reference librarian, honoring my request, brings me two

hefty directories. At Hand-Kenyon, I'm in public relations. I relate to the public by helping my bosses create corporate identity programs. Ironically, in my other, criminal, life I also describe corporate identities: with spray paint or adhesive lettering, I illuminate the true names of war contractors. Last month, the occasion for my present internment, I glued DEATH FACTORY, one large letter at a time, on the glass doors of Honeywell. It was a stupid plan: Superglue takes a good five minutes to set, contrary to its public relations claim, in freezing weather.

Myra, no doubt, would be more clever and quick if she chose to turn her ire on the bombmakers. In my case, the cops just smiled and waited until I was done, then peeled off the letters before they led me away. Ars breva.

Myra shifts her table, no mean feat, closer to the window and the heat ducts under them, making a small fort for her legs with four shopping bags and the chairs. The librarian glances over at the scraping of wooden legs on tile, but he leaves her alone. Isn't she blocking the heat ducts? I move my directories to a chair nearer hers, closer to the heat, enduring her swift suspicious stare. I smile, shrug, and bend my head to the task; I am no threat.

At Hand-Kenyon, Inc., my part is small. On days when my creative juices flow and my pen is agile, I list a dozen slogans for an upscale child care program. Brandonberry Bay: natural perfection, a multi-culture garden, tender training for tomorrow's leaders, rainbow resources. On dryer days, I research facts about potential clients, like today's dive into directories of lawyers. Midsize firms of lawyers, like all important commercial enterprises, will benefit from clear corporate identities, and will pay for them.

My fellow inmates at the workhouse collect lawyer jokes. What do you call a hundred lawyers at the bottom of the sea? A good start. Rather prejudicial, but the women have their reasons. I am learning to be tolerant of all types of people. Maybe I can understand people a little better, as I told my friend Mary at lunch today, because of my criminal tendencies. I was joking. She said, "Well, don't think you're protesting for *me*. Don't do it on my account."

"Sorry," I said, quick and flip, "I don't make exceptions." Meaning, if I was going to save the world from weapons, she'd have to be saved along with everybody else. Protesting is as close to un-

conditional love as I get. Mary, like my husband, warns me about
exercising judgment, not ending up poor and on the streets. I do
make judgments, I tell them. I take inordinate pleasure in sticking
accurate words on a flat surface, even if they disappear.

"Don't let it come close to you," Mary advised when I described
my anger at the Huber matron, at waking me at five this morning
to vacuum the guards' desk area before work. Why didn't they ever
have the men do it? I clattered about, jabbing the vacuum wand
under the desks like a weapon, sucking up paper, cigarette butts,
candy wrappers, blinking back inexplicable tears. "Anger will just
pull you back there, anger makes connections."

What seems clearest in the free air I'm breathing these days is
the individual indifference to my general concern about human
survival. I've cut a little piece off my life for them, I give what I
can afford. Is this incipient paranoia? My co-workers made jokes
for a few days about the white-bread-and-bologna bag lunches
unlovingly prepared in the jail kitchen. My boss kindly offered
sprouts from the deli downstairs. But after a week they forgot to
joke, they forget where I go to live nights and weekends.

Myra reads. She crouches over a stack of magazines, *Mademoi-
selle, Vogue, Style, Ebony.* The winter sun flickers off the glossy
pages as she turns and smooths them, hissing with pleasure. It
isn't only to be warm that she comes downtown; she is a reader,
a student of contemporary life and style.

As she reads, she croons, punctuating her soft moans with
sibilants, shaping words between her fiery lips. At last, watching
her, I see her eyes dart toward me warmly, then back to the pages,
coy, then back to me. She is inviting me in. I lean closer, inquir-
ing, to catch her words.

"Destroy them," she whispers, grinning, stroking the page,
"destroy the nigger animals."

I want to run. I don't have the time for this, I don't have the
heart for it. I don't care to speculate on the reasons, or unreason,
for her hatred. I don't want to be whirlpooled into those depths.

Can you love what you don't understand? Would Myra care if
I tried to understand? Why not consign her to the fires of her dark
opinions, or to the bottom of the sea with the lawyers? The tenuous
connection between us is snapping, as I see her bitten fingernails

hesitate on the page. We are not equals, I think, angrily, and my anger brings tears.

It's Friday. I'll go back tonight, line up at the desk to have my belongings searched, my pockets patted down. I'll have to pay the rent to the state, fifty bucks a week, in cash, for the privilege of work-jail — my privilege for having a job. Myra couldn't afford this cream-of-the-crop incarceration, not being gainfully employed. Sometimes the guards flip through my journal, idly, looking for contraband or maybe criminal intent. They haven't apparently found much of interest yet, like my heart.

Then I'll click into the locked women's wing, and open my own cell with the key worn around my neck. I'll close the curtains, because the prison rules say once the light is on, you close the curtains. What will I do next? What will I ever do?

I know irrevocably the distance between us, though Myra rages unappeased from shelter to shelter, and I, too, am a long way from home.

So I decide. Stand up. Move forward.

The Peace Terrorist

I

"**N**obody loves you when you're eleven years old."
Jacob's grandma said it often, but first she would squeeze his shoulder to say she didn't mean it. He was still eleven but now she had a variation. Nobody loves you but Jesus when you're eleven. And she didn't touch him so much; she said hugging him was like snuggling up to a rock. He was Rock Warsziniak, the bruiser, the star linebacker for the Chicago Bears.

Last summer when Jacob and his mom and his brother Jesse moved in with Grandma and Grandpa, Grandpa had welcomed him, pinching his arm: "Brown as a tree branch, not one ounce of fat!" he said.

"Yeah," Jacob's dad said, "Twig is more like it. He's going to be skinny like me." His dad was smiling but his eyes were angry. Nobody was happy packing up and moving Jacob's mom and Jesse and Jacob over to Grandma's for the separation. But Jacob's dad Jim acted like it was an insult he should have to help them move, when it wasn't his idea. Jacob's mom said the only reason he was helping was to make sure they didn't rip him off.

Grandma also used to say things would be better soon. They weren't. The latest blamefest was the peace sign Jacob had shaved into the long crew cuts Uncle Johnny gave them for Christmas. Jacob was going to make something like a Nazi-punk sign but a peace sign was more fashionable at his school. He was going to design it only for himself but Jesse had whined and pleaded until Jacob did one for his six-year-old brother, too. Jesse's was neater and rounder, since Jacob had practiced on himself. But no one liked it.

Grandma believed in peace, she said, but she thought the signs were disrespectful to Uncle Johnny who had to go to Saudi. Johnny didn't give a blip; he just said let's hope I'm home before they grow out. Grandma cried and so did his mother but they couldn't deny there was more room in the apartment when Johnny left. Now there would be even more, because Jacob was leaving.

"A change of scene," Grandma told him. "It'll be good for you." She meant good for everybody else. "It's not like you won't be back—unless you don't want to." His mom told him something different, that she and Jesse might go to live with Aunt Seal in Minneapolis too, if he liked it after a while, or maybe they would find an apartment there if his mom could transfer her Field's job to Dayton's. This way Seal could practice with a family first. Him. It was nice of Aunt Seal to offer, everyone said. They meant she was the only one in the family who got along with Jacob, probably because she wasn't around much.

She'd always been Seal, his Aunt Cecilia, with her slick black hair and her pretty dark eyes like a seal's. She had all the Italian, Grandma said, except for Jacob. Jacob inherited the dark eyes and inquisitive nose, but unlike his aunt's disappearing chin, Jacob's Polish chin stuck out into the world.

Jacob didn't mind being with Seal, except that he worried about being on the losing side. He knew his aunt was sometimes on the wrong end of things, with her letters to the editor and her barking arguments with the family. At Christmas dinner, she went on and on about peace, or she shut up and gloomed into the plates, shaking her head from side to side like a seal. Grandpa said she was always for the underdog and Seal said another war would make everybody underdogs. Grandma said somebody has to be responsible and Seal said believe me I know, with her laugh-bark, so they kind of agreed at Christmas. Grandpa told Grandma, when he didn't think Jacob could hear, that at least Seal was god-fearing and would take Jacob to Lutheran church, big whoop.

No one listened when Jacob said he'd rather stay in Chicago. He even tried to say it to the judge, only she was a lady judge and they called her a referee like on football. "Hush a minute, Jacob," his mother said. "Let her read the letters." He guessed the referee agreed with his mom because his dad never bothered to show up at the hearings. Holding them by the edge as if they'd make her fingers dirty, the judge examined the letters. His dad wrote them, to his mom and her boss at Field's and their minister at church. Jacob had seen only part of the one where Jacob drew a picture of Miss Piggy. His dad wrote his mom's name on it for a joke and wrote some other words that his mom and the judge wouldn't let Jacob see.

Maybe he could have stayed in Chicago, but just after Christmas, a week after Seal went back to Minneapolis, things fell apart. Grandpa said the bathroom night was the last straw; Jacob's dad was using Jacob to mess up the family. Everything was generally Jacob's fault. When they whispered in the kitchen, Grandma and his mom, about Grandpa's silent heart attack, they said it was stress. They meant stress from Jacob.

But it was Jesse who locked himself in the bathroom, not him. After school, they had nothing to do until their dad picked them up for supper. Jacob's mom was working extra hours because his dad wasn't paying support, but inventory after Christmas made lots of hours, so it was okay. She'd be home around midnight. The boys hung around in the apartment, not wanting to play outside in the icy courtyard, and they weren't supposed to go farther than the corner without someone bigger. Grandma said Jesse was too little to go to the playground and Jacob shouldn't go alone. Jesse was six for Christ's sake and big for his age. He'd catch up to Jacob they said if he kept going the way he was. Except he acted like a baby most of the time. Jacob could just pretend to pinch him and he'd squeal.

Their dad didn't come and didn't come and his grandma was tired of Jesse's squealing so she separated them, parking Jesse in Grandpa's chair by the television and leaving Jacob in Grandma and Grandpa's room with just a radio. Grandma told him to take a nap but he noticed his shoes made marks on the bedspread, so he decided to make a strategic circle of the room, bouncing his superball. He was supposed to bomb the targets on the opposite wall, planting one foot only on whatever furniture was in the way. It required agility, precision, and intelligence in picking his targets. He'd scored 29 in only two circles of the room, although he gave himself a 5 for hitting his mom and dad's picture between their heads, and a 10 for missing Jesus' face, catching just the left edge of his long curls. He was careful, aiming only at pictures without glass; and nothing fell. But his grandma slammed into the room, wanting to know what on earth, and confiscated his ball.

Nothing else happened except dinner which Grandma cooked because his dad didn't come but they had stupid stew with cabbage and he didn't feel like eating anyway. Jesse locked himself in the bathroom as soon as their dad rang the buzzer downstairs. Jesse said he had a stomachache. It was almost eleven and his grandma was asleep but Jacob wasn't. He ran to press the buzzer, as Jesse stumbled off the couch into the bathroom. Jacob was all for leaving him there to stew in his own juice. Jacob pictured Jesse stewing, sailing boats of cabbage leaves and paying no attention to Grandpa or anybody else telling him he was in hot water, while the greasy broth mounted to his ankles.

Grandpa tried to talk Jesse out of the bathroom, and Jacob went to wait on the landing with his dad. His dad started asking questions like if Jesse really had a stomachache and was his grandpa mean to him this week and why wouldn't Jesse come out? Patiently answering no, no, and I don't know, Jacob considered his father. Jim's thin light face looked scraped but still unshaven, his beak nose red with the sun from the loading dock, though his mother said it was drinking. He'd rather be with his father when he was quiet, just smoking and not asking questions, and when his dad's girlfriend wasn't around at his dad's place. But that was hardly ever anymore. She had to sleep with his dad and Jesse got the only couch. Jacob didn't care about that, though. He'd rather sleep on the floor anyway, the couch smelled of Jesse's pee.

He decided to go inside and say good-bye to Jesse. He leaned on the door, putting his mouth to the crack, "So long, Jesse, we're leaving now! Dad's waiting for me in the car, so good-bye!"

Naturally Jesse started yelling, but he unlocked the door, as Jacob knew he would. Jacob was going to lean against the door just until he heard the click and then jerk it open when the knob started turning, so Jesse would come out fast like a Jesse-in-the-box. He wasn't going to hurt Jesse. But Grandpa misinterpreted; he yelled, "Jacob get away from that door!" and grabbed Jacob's arm hard, as though Grandpa wasn't the one who wanted Jesse out of the bathroom in the first place.

That was when his dad went completely crackers, hollering "What's he doing to you, Jacob!" and though he stormed in and

could see nobody was doing anything to anybody, he went march-
ing up and down the hall waving his cigarette with the ashes snow-
ing and talking to the walls calling God to be his witness. Jacob
guessed he wanted the neighbors to be witness, because Mrs.
Zitkowski downstairs started knocking her broom handle on the
ceiling underneath their apartment, dah dah de dah dah! Jacob
grabbed the Comet can from the tub and answered her on the floor
tiles, dah dah! Only a little Comet spilled out and a small green
cloud went up to Jacob's nose, making him sneeze once, but it was
enough to make Jesse laugh, so his stomach must have got better.
His dad never saw it, just kept yelling at Grandpa. Grandpa was
pissed enough to tell him to shut up, Grandma was sleeping, which
was a lie because they could hear her opening and closing win-
dows, a weird action in the middle of January even to air out the
place. Jacob assumed she wasn't coming out.

Grandpa gave his dad's shoulder a small shove, or maybe Grand-
pa grabbed it to wag it in a friendly way.

"Back off, Jimmy, can't you? The kids. . . ."

But his dad slapped Grandpa's hand down and pushed on his
chest and looked like he'd do more. Jacob himself was flaking out
by this time; he grabbed Jesse's hand to pull him back in the
bathroom until his father left. Unfortunately someone grabbed
at the knob just as Jacob was closing the door and Jacob's finger
was the one that got jammed. He couldn't help shrieking.

His dad said it was Grandpa's fault, and Grandpa didn't know.
Grandpa stopped looking angry and looked old. He asked Jacob
to move the finger, which was red as hell, so he didn't want to.
His dad said the finger was probably broken. It wasn't though.
His dad said it was too late to go out now, and he had to leave,
he wasn't feeling well.

Grandpa said, "Go on, you already started making a night of
it, to judge by your breath; go on home!"

Jacob's dad stood there with his fists clenched as though he'd
like to start up the fight again, but he finally turned and went out.
As soon as the apartment door banged, like magic Grandma ap-
peared with ice cubes wrapped in a towel and told Jacob to hold
it. He didn't want to, but he had to admit the cold helped a little.
Jesse just kept sucking his own thumb as though he was the one
who got hurt.

That was the way Jacob's life went that winter, picked up one place and put down in another, like mail. He had to go to Aunt Seal's. That was the way it was, he had no say in the matter.

II

Aunt Seal met him at the airport the day after the real war started, the day after we bombed Baghdad. It was a strange feeling, being in the air and thinking of bombs. The night the bombs dropped, Mrs. Zitkowski even came to their door during supper. It was the first time he'd seen her in person and she didn't look like a shriveled prune, the way he'd pictured her. She was fat, or anyway coming out of her clothes in places where a serious-looking baby on her hip pulled at them. "Turn on your television!" she said, "It started." He didn't know she had a baby either, and maybe it was Mr. Z who pounded on the ceiling all the time. Only the mailbox name just said Mrs. Zitkowski. Grandma didn't let the boys stay up to watch the bombs, she said Jacob had a long trip tomorrow. Jacob was thinking maybe his flight would be canceled, but Grandma said she hardly thought so, the war was a long way away.

It was Thursday night, January seventeen, and Jacob was flying, aimed at Minneapolis. He watched the lights sliding below, on and on, bright stones spaced evenly on a dark table. Most were pale yellow, a few sulfurous orange. Baghdad must have looked like that from the air, except maybe they had blackouts. He wondered. They didn't know when it was going to be, but our president warned them. He told them it was going to happen. Jacob couldn't see any tall buildings; it must be neighborhoods below.

"Hey, you want to trade seats, or what?" the man next to him groused. To see, Jacob had to lean over the lap of a large man who had hogged the window. It was a dumb question, Jacob thought, because the seatbelt sign was on. But the man took charge; he unsnapped the belts, lifted the hinged arm between them, hitched himself up and let Jacob scoot under his legs to the window seat. The stewardess never saw them.

Jacob was most interested in the blue moving necklaces, especially a long curving one whose jewels winked on and off, automobile lights under spiky shadows of trees. The long necklace was the road next to the dark Minnesota River, or maybe it was the Mississippi there. Near the airport, the Minnesota joined the Mississippi in a Y whose right arm climbed into St. Paul, before the Mississippi swooped down to meet the St. Croix from the north and made the border of Minnesota and Wisconsin and Iowa and even Illinois and way down to New Orleans. He looked at the map last night when Grandma didn't let him watch the war. He could be a pilot, he had a great sense of direction: Jacob Warsziniak, decorated bomber pilot of World War III. He narrowed his eyes at the necklace below and aimed carefully.

Then the necklace of cars rushed toward him, the noise accelerating until his ears could hardly stand it. For a brief moment he imagined the metal roof of a car and heads oblivious to the missile racing down to meet them, the parents in the front, arguing about where to go, a couple of kids in the back seat. There was a muffled shriek as the plane's engines reversed, then a calm drift past the focused lights of the runway. They made it, they were down.

Jacob hadn't had time to imagine an enemy. At first, it seemed like there were no people, only lights — nobody cooking late dinners or going to the movies or Burger King or to meet someone. Of course he knew they were real people under the plane, under the winking lights, under the roofs of cars. Maybe one of the blue jewels had been Aunt Seal. A little dizzy from concentrating so hard, he stood shakily on the seat to pull down his backpack from the overhead compartment. His seatmate had stood up before the plane stopped rolling, and was gone; everyone was in a hurry tonight. The stewardess at the door gave him a bright good-bye, staring at some point over his eyes. He looked behind himself but the plane was empty.

Grandma had told him Aunt Seal couldn't come to the concourse because of security. The airlines were afraid of terrorists. That was wise, he thought, he could be a spy from Chicago bringing in stuff, some message from headquarters.

Aunt Seal would wait at the baggage claim on the bottom floor, and the crinkle of the claim check in his shirt pocket reassured him. Still, he wished, as his feet felt the wobble and creak of the metal of the accordion gangway, for a glimpse of her head craning over a crowd looking for him. The concourse was nearly deserted, and of the people bored or busy walking past him, none suspected his name, Warsziniak the Spy. They wouldn't even look at him, unless he shouted hi! to startle them. He didn't.

He forgot to ask directions to the baggage claim, absorbed in counting the number of bars on this concourse. Every other waiting area seemed to be next to a bar or snack shop. Of course he'd been in bars with his father, but not such fancy ones, with blonde counters and red leather high seats with backs. His father's bars were noisier, too. Here, the television wasn't showing any sports, just news. The people stood around staring, with drinks in their hands or forgotten on the bar, at the screen, and listened like they were in church. No one spoke.

Outside one lounge, Jacob watched as the television image shifted from a serious announcer in a suit to a monster, some kind of humanoid or droid with a huge insect head with goggle eyes and a snout. It was obviously a mask, but somehow he knew he shouldn't laugh. Then the monster lifted his head off and he was a regular reporter talking about nerve gas. The reporter was actually in a bomb shelter. The shelter was really an ordinary room; the camera panned to tape on the window and door. Two kids played on the floor in a corner. Then one of the kids looked up at the camera and his mouth drooped and he looked kind of like Jesse; the other kid was even smaller.

"Jacob!" Aunt Seal was trying to pick him up and squeeze and yell at him all at once. With her was a man in an airport police uniform, so Jacob didn't know if they were under arrest, or what.

They didn't let him watch any more television, but he didn't mind — his eyes were scratchy and watery from watching too much. It turned out that a steward was supposed to hand Jacob over to his aunt like he was a package, but someone had got the wrong flight number and he'd escaped. Then they both had to go with the policeman through a metal scanner. The man mumbled into a little radio, but then he let them go to the baggage claim by themselves. "Don't get lost any more, sonny, hear?" he said. As if Jacob really was lost, instead of ignored in an airport screwup, he was going to say, but Seal kept squeezing his hand.

Jacob's red suitcase rode lonely around the carousel inside a fence, waiting for him. No one even checked his pass when he went through the barred turnstile. "Some security," he grumbled. "I could have *anything* in here." Aunt Seal ruffled his hair, but he noticed she looked around quickly.

By the time they pulled up in Aunt Seal's driveway, it was nearly midnight. He was supposed to be registered next day, Seal said, so she scooted him into his room next to the kitchen, with the covers turned back on one twin bed. Jesse could have the other one when he came. Great, he thought, just get my own room and look forward to having Jesse in it. But the picture of the taped room in his mind faded a little, and he drank some milk with Seal.

He liked the way the snow lit up his bedroom, after Seal clicked off the kitchen light. Seal's house was small, one story with three tiny bedrooms, just enough. His window faced a back yard, with a spruce tree that was gathering white by the minute, from fat flakes that glittered like sidewalk mica when they landed. The snow didn't do that in Chicago. Or maybe it did on late cold nights without wind or so much pollution. He'd have to check sometime. If they lived here they'd probably visit Grandma and Grandpa pretty often. That would be okay. When the flakes filled up Seal's footprints by the bird feeder, then he'd get in bed. But it took too long; his eyes were scratchy again.

No wonder he was crabby the next morning. Even though it was Friday and the semester had just begun, you think they'd let him sleep in for one day? No, he had to be wrapped up and shipped off to school so he wouldn't miss any of the stupid lessons. He had to go through his stuff and pick out the least dorky sweat-shirt and then change because Seal said it was hot in the classrooms and he should layer, wear a thin one underneath. After school, she said, he could shop for some nonholey socks and boots.

It was too much. He threw himself face down on his bed; no way. No way was he going to drag along behind Aunt Seal in some stupid suburb mall, full of yuppie banners and crud boxes of ferns and fertilizer, which was shit anyway, wasn't it? He worked himself up to tell her so, but when he looked up she wasn't there and he smelled the hot sharp smell of pancakes.

Seal must have ripped off a funhouse mirror for the bathroom; the nerd looking back at him looked swollen as an apple under his skin. He looked like he was about to whine or say something snotty to someone who'd want to at least hit him like his dad or even once or twice lately his mother. He could make her cry just like his dad did by the things he said. He had a way with words lately.

Maybe Seal would too if he was snotty enough. Probably she'd just send him back, like a package. "I'm a goddam package!" he yelled at the mirror, astounded at the red-apple ferocity of his face.

"What?" Seal was at the door, and their eyes met in the mirror. He looked away, then back, horrified as Seal pushed her nose flat with two thumbs and with her little fingers pulled her eyes into slits and stuck out her tongue. "Hey Jake, can you do that?" He couldn't help giggling even if she did think he was some kind of baby, needing to be entertained for Christ's sake.

Breakfast wasn't bad though the cakes were a little black around the edges, from the fooling around in the mirror. But then Seal informed him that she expected him to do the sock shopping. It wasn't far, she said, just three blocks down, and not a mall, it was a funky seconds store. She said she hated shopping, every time she passed a mirror she wanted to do this — she pushed her nose in — and he couldn't help laughing until his stomach hurt. And then she gave him a pair of sunglasses to be incognito if he wanted. He'd cruise with the glasses and if a saleslady pestered him he'd say not just yet, ma'am. Should he say ma'am? Not just yet, thanks, that was better.

But at school the teacher asked him to take off the glasses while she introduced him so everybody could see his eyes.

"They're pink," he cracked, "I'm an albino!" and there were a few laughs. The black kid Phil at the next desk got more laughs when he said, "Yeah, so am I."

Phil and another black kid and Jacob were the only three who had relatives in Desert Shield. Everybody in the class was supposed to write to somebody in Desert Shield. Only now it was Desert Storm, Ms. Ward the teacher told them; Jacob thought the name was stupid because it probably meant a sandstorm, and how could you bomb in sandstorms? On the television before the bombs fell, the land looked like snow, like a white empty beach at night. Anyway the bombs were probably like lightning and there was no lightning in desert storms. Or was there? He'd have to write and ask Uncle Johnny.

Except that he gave the job of writing to Uncle Johnny to the girl Abby. He hadn't meant to say anything about Johnny; it was the teacher's fault. This teacher was a jerk sometimes, as most of his teachers had been. She made such a big deal that Abby would have to write to a senator, because Abby's mother had called the school and said she was a social worker and she was worried that her daughter and other young children were writing and forming relationships with soldiers. So Abby was the only one who had to write to a senator, while the rest of the class got to write to soldiers.

So Jacob announced that Abby could have his Uncle Johnny; maybe her mother wouldn't mind her writing if it wasn't to a stranger, and Jacob would write to the senator. Jacob had a couple of things to say to a senator, anyway. Abby had red-brown hair and looked mad all the time she was in the classroom.

"Don't you want to write your uncle, Jacob?" He told Ms. Ward he'd written already, which was half a lie but he'd been thinking about what he'd write to him on the plane.

"Abby. Would you and Jacob work on a joint letter to the senator." She didn't make it a question. "And you could think, too, about what you might write to Jacob's uncle." Abby didn't look at her, but she muttered something out the window.

"Abby, we speak out in this classroom." Ms. Ward's voice had prickles in it that made Jacob want to grit his teeth. Abby said, fairly loud for a girl, "I said my mother said they could die. The people we're writing to could die."

"They're not the only ones," Jacob said, but not very loud, because Ms. Ward just went on talking to Abby. He stuck his hand in the air, waiting for the teacher to stop talking.

"We know your mother has strong beliefs about peace and that's important to all of us, even though we may not agree with them, isn't it class? And we protect those freedoms, don't we? Yes, Jacob?"

"Bombs kill kids, too," he informed her. He meant in Iraq and maybe Israel, where the taped-up room on television was, but a nerdy girl in front of him waved her hand in his face and said, "Teacher, are we going to die?"

Ms. Ward spent the rest of the time until recess explaining with maps how far away Iraq was, and that the bombs couldn't reach Minneapolis, for Christ's sake. Jacob was paired up with Abby for most of the day, which he really didn't mind because she fit his mood. She was mad at everyone especially her mother and Ms. Ward. If her mother or Ms. Ward said the P word once more to her she'd spit in class.

"What P word, piss?" It was all he could think of but he couldn't imagine Ms. Ward saying it. He and Abby were standing in a snow fort on the playground that they'd fixed up with new snow from last night. The temperature had risen so that by mid-morning the snow was decent for packing. Abby told him they weren't supposed to throw snowballs during school, but sometimes people did. He scooped and packed some spares, just in case. Abby's cheeks were so red they looked chapped, but she really looked better when she laughed.

"Nooo. It just *sounds* like a bad word. PEACE!" she shrieked. A bunch of kids waiting in line to go inside looked over at them. A big kid, an eighth grader, yelled back, "Okay, okay, we surrender!" Then the kids walked inside holding their hands in the air, making fun of them.

But Abby thought it was cool. "We're peace terrorists!" And she wouldn't go inside until they had stomped out a peace sign in the snow under their room's windows. They kept up the peace theme all day. At lunch, Jacob ordered peace soup when he saw the putrid pale green mush that was the choice du jour, though he hated peas. The cafeteria lady glanced at him suspiciously; "It's broccoli," she told him. He took it anyway. Abby selected the vegetarian plate, mounding mashed potatoes and vegetables to form another peace sign. They shared the food; Jacob was hungry.

In the afternoon they had to write to the senator. They wrote, "We are two eleven-year-olds from Chicago and Minneapolis who don't want the war to continue. Too many people on all sides will be killed." Jacob wanted to put in, 'Bombs kill kids, too,' but Ms. Ward was monitoring them and she didn't think the tone was respectful. She gave them a B for the letter, though. All in all, it wasn't a bad day.

Sunday was the best, though, even if he and Seal had to go to church. On Saturday Jacob said he'd rather not, if Aunt Seal didn't mind. He admitted Grandma wanted him to go and pray to Jesus, but if Grandma thought you could pray anywhere, what was the point? It wasn't for kids anyway. He hadn't thought Seal would pressure him, but she did. She said he might not understand now, but later he could take comfort from church. She said *she* took comfort, especially when the world didn't make sense. He said he would be more comfortable staying home and he didn't mind.

But she informed him that he was going to stay home for a little while today, because she was going to visit some friends of hers in jail who were in because of peace demonstrations.

"I'd rather go with you today," Jacob pleaded, "couldn't I go there instead of to church?"

Absolutely not, she told him, kids weren't allowed unless they had a parent inside, and then only special hours once a week. He couldn't even wait in the car for Christ's sake, even if he hid under a blanket so the guard at the gate didn't see him.

"Would they let me in if you were in jail? And how come you're not, didn't you demonstrate?"

Seal didn't know about the first question. Then she told him: "I've already been in jail, Jacob. Right after the sit-in, after Christmas, I pleaded guilty because I knew you were coming and I couldn't risk more time. See, you get more time if you go through a trial and say what you did was right. I wanted to get the sentence out of the way."

He didn't understand. She didn't tell Grandma or anyone. Seal didn't even send him a postcard from jail. Then she said it was no goddamn adventure, she even used the swear word. They didn't have a good relationship on Saturday morning for goddamn sure.

Saturday night was a little better. In the afternoon while Seal was gone, he stomped out stuff, m-f war, damn Saddam and other words on the sidewalk in front of the house, then shoveled, dribbling the massacred hate words onto the snowbanks along with the dog pee. He was going to finish it off with a peace sign on the lawn, but the snow looked swept clean, not even a wind ripple, so he decided to leave it.

Seal told him he'd done a great job — even the driveway! which she hadn't asked him to do. He shrugged, admitting he had pretty good arms. They were aching, though; he wasn't used to it. After dinner, he let her beat him once at Chinese checkers, and she told him a few things about jail without his asking. She said almost everyone in there was young and skinny but her. He asked about the food; she said it was all right if you liked white bread and potatoes, which of course he did. So he wondered what the bad part was for her.

"Not having any choices, I guess. No, the worst part was being with women with less choice about what they do."

"Kids don't have any choice," he told her. Her dark eyes were bright for a second, and she looked away.

"They do, Jacob. They still do — only it's hard to see what the choices are, sometimes."

"Not important ones," he mumbled, looking down at his new socks, which were an interesting shade of green the saleslady tried to talk him out of. He could tell Seal liked them because she asked to borrow his sunglasses to look at them. But he knew she was humoring him, and he knew kids didn't have any say about what mattered, like whether a bomb was going to be sent at them. You just had to be on the right side.

By Sunday morning, he was resigned to spending a boring hour. Seal promised that after church he could vegetate and watch the Super Bowl, though what, she said, a nice peace terrorist like him could enjoy about a bunch of cauliflower heads making themselves into chopped liver she'd never understand. Actually, he never did watch the game. He couldn't wait to tell Jesse what happened.

Ten minutes into the service, the pastor said, "I ask all the children and anyone who's a child at heart to gather around." Since Seal had told Jacob what to expect, he wasn't too surprised that a few kids and no adults ambled up the nave and sat down around the skirted minister. Jacob wasn't thrilled about it, but Seal said the pastor sometimes gave the kids little presents, like chewing gum or a Bible card. He wondered if there was a choice, but from the looks of Pastor Nusswandt, he doubted it.

Pastor Nusswandt was large, blond, and kind of young for a minister. Jacob thought he wouldn't want him falling on him, as the pastor leaned forward from the altar step to pin each kid in the circle with his pale blue eyes, scowling as he did.

"Do any of you think Jesus was a wimp? You've seen the pictures, haven't you — the long hair, the gentle expression?"

Jacob didn't particularly think long hair was wimpy, but he didn't feel like bringing that up at the moment. In fact, nobody admitted they thought the Jesus pictures looked wimpy. Only about five kids had come up and most of them were small.

The pastor leaned back, satisfied. He talked about driving bad men out of the temple with a whip and how in His day that took anger and courage, too. Then he was talking about Saddam, and Jesus giving his life and our soldiers risking their lives and the minutes stretched on. Jacob arranged his brain to be back in the airplane, thinking about Johnny. It was a half hour before they landed, and the evening came quickly. Night deepened over farms and highways as he watched. Clouds slid under the plane and hid the land, clouds turning blue and deeper blue, like lumpy snow, then like blue-tinged hills to shelter the soldiers, then nothing, black, nothing but his own scared face reflected in the window.

The pastor told them to stand up for Jesus, and released them. By this time, bulletins crackled, and the congregation was generally coughing and moving its feet. Back in their pew, Aunt Seal's face was white, and her hands clenched the seat like it was about to take off.

Fortunately, no adult sermon was scheduled, only a hymn sing. Pastor Nusswandt suggested — his nod to the organist made it not a suggestion — that they begin with "Onward Christian Soldiers." Seal groaned, but she opened her hymnal. She whispered, "Remember, it's *spiritual* foes!" Jacob knew the song. It was about taking action, and Jesus leading with banners and all that.

But the pastor stopped them after the first verse and made them sing it again. He said he knew it wasn't their tradition to be rousers with hymns but they shouldn't sit on their dignity now, they should remember the boys — and girls — over there and "Get into it, people. Show them how, children!" He started with a low and offkey "FOR-ward into ba-attle," marching his feet up and down and staring straight at Jacob, who swallowed something between singing and a throatlump that tasted terrible. He understood then that Aunt Seal was wrong: they weren't singing about spiritual foes at all. Pastor Nusswandt's congregation sang against a real enemy with human faces.

Bombs kill kids too, didn't they know? He thought about the kid in the taped-up room, a kid like Jesse and Abby and even himself, waiting for something to fall. Jacob knew beyond any teaching that he didn't want to sing that song.

He decided what to do; it was his choice. Clicking loud on the linoleum floor, Jacob tramped down the nave and up the side aisle, swinging his arms, goose-stepping enthusiastically past the pastor, who stared and dropped a couple of notes. Still marching, but faster, Jacob paraded back to his aunt. There he marched in place, holding out his hand as if to share the peace but looking desperately at the back door. As he knew she would, Aunt Seal grasped his hand and walked with him out of the church. The last notes they heard, 'the cross of Jee-sus,' stretched thin and reedy behind them, as one by one the voices dropped away.

Diver

Seal is a dumpster diver. Not that this occupation is her need, nor is it her only profession, or else the clergy on the Homeless Alliance Board would not delight in holding her up to their congregations: "See what can be done with simple tools." She is never sure whether they mean the recycled goods, or herself. Probably both.

Out of her hearing, she knows (she has her sources) that they comment wryly on her bolder incursions into the depths and back alleys behind supermarkets and pizza parlors. Like *Cecilia,* they'd say, emphasizing Seal's real name in a commentary on some less savory aspect of environmental activism. She is become a byword to the nations.

But her finds are practical, and organizational. No thrift shop fashion accessories to brag on at church suppers or middle-class teas, with a conspiratorial whisper, "Just six dollars, and barely worn!" Seal's treasures are a collection of outerwear dumped in her washer two or three times — if the clothes make it through, she'll deliver them to the Free Store. Leather shoes and boots, steamed, aired, disinfected, prodded and polished to a matte glow — they can be reheeled by Dave the Leather Man, so that a drop-in at the Homeless Alliance Center might find the right size. Her boot stock is nearly gone this wet long winter; she has to keep checking the bins.

And furniture — amazing what people will throw away that is still serviceable: cabinets, chairs, a lot of wooden chairs with maybe a rung missing, or a padded seat that needs restitching. If it were spring or summer, not bitter cold, end of February, she could salvage such gorgeous floral arrangements behind the funeral parlor! It wasn't true, but a rumor spread by malicious Pastor Micah, that he'd seen a delicate wreath in Seal's living room still wearing a banner "For Our Beloved Mother."

Food. She's on a first-name basis with produce managers at three chain stores and the co-op in her neighborhood. Too much red tape to manage delivery of aging surplus to the larger social service agencies, but she has a small cadre of gleaners who make good use of what she can pick up. It isn't enough, a drop in the bucket, really. If she could only find a direct way to homeless families — no, with no cooking facilities, what would Jenna and Julie and Rainy do with thirty heads of broccoli?

The alley has been safe for her. It was years ago, miles away, that a dumpster was fatal to a homeless sleeper — a transient, unfamiliar no doubt with Minnesota plummeting temperatures. But she thought about him sometimes, as she swung back the black heavy lids. Inadequately bundled up? Nothing to make a nest there — drunk, careless, injured — did he have any inkling how deep he was going, as the cold came through and through. . . .

This morning it was a dead cat. Seal hadn't meant to pass the dumpster with Rainy, but Seal was going to bring her home, find mittens, and the alley was on their way.

Rainy is difficult. "A crack child," the Center supervisor told her. Seal doesn't believe the quick diagnosis. From what she understands, a placenta does a better job of protecting babies than society does after they get here. But the label means Rainy has a place to go this morning, and Seal has the task of delivering her to the preschool Class for Disadvantaged at Saint Stephen's. Nevertheless, Rainy won't talk to her.

"Come on, Sunshine," Seal coaxes, crouching, trying to fasten Rainy's coat zipper, "Tell me your name? It must be Sunshine, those pretty yellow bows all over?"

Rainy's crinkly hair is damp from combing, twisted into six neat pigtails; the bow-barrettes have seen brighter days, their gold color flaked and dingy, but there are six of them. Rainy's head dips, butting Seal in the nose, and the little girl mumbles a word. It sounds like "broke." Rainy's mother Jenna comes in from an office behind the day room, where she's filled out permission for Rainy to be taken to school.

"Her name's Rainy, just the *opposite*." Jenna shakes her head at the girl, "You go with the lady, now. You can button your *own* coat." Jenna speaks loudly, enunciating the words, but Rainy doesn't seem hard of hearing. Her mother explains, "The social worker tells me she understands better if you talk right at her, and let her help herself."

And indeed Rainy's fingers are nimble on the three snaps left on her coat. The zipper is broken, Seal hadn't seen that. Then Rainy stands stark still, her arms stiff at her side, her lip curling in a look that on any face but one so small would be scorn.

"You're not going before a firing squad, Rainy, just to school," Seal banters. No response. She takes the limp tiny hand in her mittened one, and leads her unresisting into the snowy day.

Snow has been falling since dawn, fine as mist, coating the grimy persistent piles of shoveled snow and ice fencing streets and walks, piles nearly head-high for Rainy. They are a pair, Seal sees in the dim shop windows along Franklin. Their reflections in the winter-grimed glass show a large and a small yard bag scooting along, yard bags with legs. To herself, Seal looks lumpish and formidable, towing her small charge through a white haze.

Seal decides they'll stop by her house, which is almost on the way to the school, and find another jacket: she's sure she has one Rainy's size, not so drab. The dirty beige and broken-zippered coat is probably a boy's, several sizes too large, since it covers Rainy's bare knees. Jenna had expressed concern about their walking, and Stevie, the Center director, assured her it wasn't far. But those bare knees, Seal thought. Seal didn't own a car.

"Stupid little bubbles," she'd say to Jacob, "farting pollution all over Creation, for what? Just to get one person to someplace he could've got to easier on the bus."

"Buses pollute," Jacob would answer. "Buses stink. And not everybody works where you can get to on the bus." He had a point.

"Bad planning," she'd close off the discussion.

"Rainy, you ever had a car?" Seal bends her head toward the little girl, whose weight against her arm is continuous, though Seal plods short steps and slow, trying to match them to Rainy's. She glances back at their footprints, each pair of her galoshes' prints alongside three or four smaller prints — not too bad. Rainy appears to shake her head; at least the yellow pompom on top of her snow hat wobbles.

"Well, don't ever get one." This is patently unfair, but no objection is forthcoming. Rainy trudges, her cool hand obedient in Seal's, without looking up. She breaks away once on Franklin, trots a few steps to Eddy's Cafe next to the alley, where she pounds on the window furiously. The window is grimy with splashed slush, and Seal has to mop the recaptured hand with a handkerchief, shaking her head apologetically at Eddy, who looks bemused and sleepy behind his empty counter. Eddy raises one hand from his coverall apron, still spotless this early, though otherwise the mound of him resembles the mounds in front of his cafe. He likes his own cooking, Eddy does.

"Bet we woke *him* up, didn't we, Rainy? That's Eddy. He's a good guy, makes a great fried-egg sandwich. You hungry?"

Rainy wobbles her pompom, decidedly this time, and Seal remembers that the family would have been given a light breakfast at the shelter. Still, maybe she can give Rainy a glass of juice before school. And mittens.

"Tell you what, Sunshine. This alley is a shortcut to my house. We'll hustle through here and get you all fixed up and pretty for school." Seal plans to have just a peek in the dumpster, too, although summertime is better for clothes. She never knows what is likely to be down there.

Last month in this very spot she was practically accosted by two bright yellow chairs, their enamel gloss barely chipped, perched on the four-foot snowbank next to the dumpster. Of course she claimed them, steamed home through a January snow like today's with a chair on each arm. She had such a time — that was after the big snows and Jacob's igloo, before people chopped or trampled paths through the piles — she crested each snow bank at the street corners like a wintry but gaily painted excursion boat. Jacob said she looked like a boat.

The chairs still sit in the bay window of her small stucco house, a conversational pair, never used now, for conversations, anyway. A yellow party hat Jacob refused to wear on his twelfth birthday sits on a table between them.

Jacob is gone. She's failed as usual to make a family. Her twelve-year-old nephew left to try again with his mom and brother in

Chicago. Jacob was with her only a month, a time that dizzied her with its energy and speed. Seal lives alone, which she prefers. She suffers often enough from free-floating love — so intense for the world of everyone that she will moan sometimes with frustration, and it is difficult to pour the coffee for her clients, the homeless ones, even placing the cup on a flat surface. Emotion comes unbidden, no sense to it. Seal tends to spiritual randiness, sporadic but unpredictable, indiscriminate affection for humanity; she is afraid that it shows in her eyes and in her laughter at grown people.

Revealing such emotion is intrusive, she thinks, in her context of social life and work, even dangerous in these times of random muggings. Therefore she pulls curtains over her features, as she pulls the drapes of her living room closed in the morning when she leaves, so the quiet rooms won't be apparent from the street. Seal's house, a remnant from a divorce several years old, is empty again.

Or as empty as the clutter of about-to-be-repaired seconds and stray furniture will allow. Even during the weeks Jacob stayed, his room was storage for clothes in process, heading toward washing and mending and the Free Store.

Jacob helped out, until he became bored. He was best at sorting. "Cool. Dud. Hot! Okay . . . " His eyes squinting and his outstretched hand rocking in air, the fashion pundit was uncertain, could go either way.

Seal held up a multicolored fluorescent tank top, size 20, expostulating. "Cool?! Not too garish?"

"Gah-rish?" he hooted, giving it an all-Chicago emphasis. "Man, I'd like to see those gah-rish headlights!"

"Jacob, where do you get that language? Headlights," she meant to grin, be lighthearted.

But he was on the defensive, still, after several weeks — at least on some subjects.

"Headlights ain't a bad word," he said sullenly.

"Oh, I know." She gave him a light push on the shoulder. He sniffed, though, and busied himself with a pile of clothes.

That was another thing; when he'd come, he'd been angry every day. Now — or before he left — he couldn't seem to argue with her without his eyes tearing up; and when he left on the train he hugged her too long and hard, his blond head buried in her jacket front and leaving spots. Then he jumped on the Amtrak without looking back.

"Be safe," she said aloud, because he couldn't hear her.

She worried about safety. She was obsessive. Seal was just like her grandmother. In the stuffy apartment near the Illinois Central tracks, Granny would loom over twelve-year-old Seal at night, her eyes madly reflecting the light from the I.C. train whining up the tracks. Teetering at the end of the double bed, Granny would grab her ankles, or pin her arms to the bed. "Don't fall!"

"Granny wake up!" Seal would plead, when her heart stopped knocking. "I'm not falling!"

Granny's eyes were open but she was asleep. She was a real sleepwalker, the only one Seal had ever known. Seal's mom said once they took Granny to a psychiatrist to get to the bottom of it, but she never went back. Granny said the man asked too many personal questions; she wanted no part of it.

Now Seal was just as crazy. She'd inherited the worry about children, the conviction that something bad was likely to happen if you relaxed your vigilance.

After Jacob's first school day, Seal had changed her schedules at the Alliance to be home after school. That day, when she was working noon to seven at the drop-in center, she'd asked him to call and he hadn't. Three, three-thirty, and she'd called him. No answer. Four o'clock. It was January; even on sunny days the snow turned blue at four-thirty and the blue shadows hid the slick treachery underfoot. If no one passed, Jacob could be lying there on the front walk alone — how long before his thermal core dipped below the critical point?

Or if someone tried to stop him — Seal looked around wildly at the Alliance clients, curled in chairs in the lounge, alone in their morbid self-concerns, cradling coffee in isolation or muttering to a newspaper. Someone like any one of them out on the street might accost Jacob, push him for change. Her clients were islands, mutely miserable as people who wait on winter nights in bus shelters, shoulders hunched, past expectancy.

She had to get hold of herself. She closed up early, after washing the cups and coffeepot, giving the men vouchers for a free snack at Eddy's. They grumbled, but luckily only four men were in that afternoon, and these all had shelter vouchers for the night.

"Jacob!" She fumbled with the doorkey, her fingers numb after the three-block walk. Then the door was open and Jacob stood there, a popcorn bowl in his hand; in a moment, it was wedged between them, digging into her solar plexus as she bear-hugged him.

"Jesus, Aunt Seal, don't crush the kernels!"

"Where have you been?" Even as she blurted it, she was laughing with relief at the absurdity of her fears.

Except that the dark part of her knows they aren't absurd. She knows the streets, to an extent. Safety is relative. She never wants him to be alone.

He mumbled that he lost the number at the Alliance, he was sorry. He didn't know if he should answer the phone. In Chicago, if he was by himself, he wouldn't. Seal was euphoric with relief, but the question gave her pause. Seal and Jacob decided he should say, who's calling please, and if he didn't know the name, he should say, Seal can't come now (she's in the bathroom feeding the cobra, she's doing her karate, she's downstairs at the rifle range). They sat on the floor beside the flickering television and giggled, making up stories where Seal could be.

Instead of right beside him. It seemed Seal was checking the window every ten minutes from behind the drapes if Jacob was outside. She pretended to doze in the armchair if he'd been driven to a school event at night, but really she couldn't help listening for the crunch of car wheels. Oh, she was crazy all right, and worried herself near thin pretending not to be.

Now children of the Homeless Alliance are not her favorite assignment. Her palms sweat with worry until she has delivered them to the appropriate office, or school, or she has finished a daycare stint. Yet afterward her heart is lightened by the memory of their soft comments, and she sees more clearly, as though their newer eyes have swept the surroundings clean for her. It's the relief, she tells herself, of seeing them safe to the next piece of land.

"Down here, Sunshine." She tugs Rainy's unresisting body into the partial shelter of the alley. Flipping back the heavy metal cover of the dumpster needs two hands, so she has to drop Rainy's. "Hang on to my coat a minute, Sunshine, if you want to. I'm just going to peek in here."

A small sound from Rainy could be fear, or a question. "Just a second, sweetheart, I just want to see . . ." Nothing. The usual ordered lumps of black plastic, strangled with twistems at the top, an old smell of rotting food, faint because frozen. A box half-filled with a curl of dirty blanket and a gray matted fur, hat? Rainy wraps her hands in Seal's coat front, begging incomprehensibly, her face contorted.

"Okay, okay, but there's nothing to see." Seal lifts the girl, a lightweight, really, to the edge of the bin. "Nothing, see?"

Rainy squirms, gripping the edge, twists her lithe body as though she'll dive in. "Key!" Rainy says clearly, pointing, reaching, as Seal sees it, the stiff gray form in the box, tip of a pink tongue protruding from a silver and back snout, but otherwise peaceful as sleep.

"Oh. Oh, honey, no, he's dead. Kitty's dead." She pries Rainy's hands from the icy bin, and eases her down. Seal forgets to close the lid, leaves open the bin with its gone scraps of day, daily bread and meat and litter and cat remnant. But Rainy hits the dumpster hard with her fist and starts to cry. As Seal crouches to comfort her, wondering what to say, Rainy's face changes. It empties of emotion as though she's decided to let it seep out. Too much to think about. Rainy's whole body seems drained of energy. Her hand is limp in Seal's but she doesn't pull back now, and they walk steadily the two blocks to the house.

The snow decides to fatten, falling with authority, straight down. Snow Jacob would enjoy, a watery pack to it that would crown the igloo they'd almost finished before the January mild weather turned to a vicious arctic blast and kept them in. Jacob had hoped for a night he could sleep in it; Seal had temporized, saying they'd study up on the Inuit, see what it took to survive the cold.

His enthusiasm passed before the cold snap had, but the igloo still stands, the shell of it — shorter as the longer sunny days walk from the solstice, but the shell is still a good four feet tall, half curved over. The back half is an unlidded bowl of snow, curving gray-white walls Jacob had shaped, packing and pouring, to encircle himself.

Rainy points to the strange white shape, inquiring, as they turn into Seal's front walk. "My nephew, Jacob, was building it. Igloo," she forms the words in a smile and a lip-purse, i-gloo, "a little snow house. Would you like to go inside?" A crawl space opens from a forsythia bush into the entrance, the only way in. But Rainy backs away.

"Okay, let's go into *my* house and find you a pretty coat."

The living room is dim and chilly. Seal had, of course, set back the thermostat, not knowing she'd be back so soon, and left the blinds drawn except for the bay window. If the sun had come out, this was its place. Rainy makes a beeline for the yellow chairs and sits primly down in her coat, waiting, her feet stuck straight ahead. A piece of slush plops onto the carpet; Rainy regards it, impassive.

"Oh Sunshine, we can at least get those wet socks and shoes off! What are we thinking, no boots in this snow?"

Guiltily, Seal rummages in the boot box in Jacob's room, knowing she should have checked before they left the center. No, first things first. She grabs a towel from the bathroom, no, not the damp one from her shower this morning, but Jacob's. It *was* Jacob's, hung now creased neatly in thirds, on the rack where Jacob would never leave it. With careful, clumsy-feeling fingers she pries at the soggy knots and loops in Rainy's sneaker shoelaces. How did the little girl manage to pull them so tight? "Rainy, hold still! I can't get them off if you bounce your legs like that!" Seal peels off one dripping sock, then the other; almost magenta, these wrinkled and stuck-with-damp-and-lint extremities.

She rubs Rainy's legs briskly, then leaves the towel draped over them, tucking it under Rainy's hips. "There, now you're a grandma, a little old lady taking a trip on a cruise ship!" Seal is thinking of a deck chair; Rainy won't know what she's talking about, how silly. But Seal sees teeth. "Sunshine, are you laughing at me? You *can* smile!" The grin stretches on until, embarrassed, Seal looks away.

The child seems to be suppressing a tremble. She shivers then stops, like a small overexcited terrier. "I'd best check out the coat situation." Seal turns away, hoping she hasn't overstimulated the poor tyke. Back in Jacob's room, in a boxed clutter of children's winter wear, she finds a poly-filled jacket, a bright turquoise with red trim, and a pair of red boots approximately Rainy's size. Rainy has already stripped off the oversized wool coat and, hobbling to the bedroom in her deck-chair skirt, she dumps the reject into the box.

"That's right. Off with the old scratchy stuff, on with the new. Consumer society, right, jumping jack?" For Rainy, clutching her towel, is bounding legless in excited mermaid circles. Seal rummages for a pair of red leggings; without the long coat, Rainy will need them. A pair of Jacob's wool-blend socks, the green fluorescent ones that hurt her heart he'd forgotten them, complete the ensemble.

Seal lays the bright collection on Jacob's bed. A too-familiar sense of something lost, a small drawing pain in her abdomen, nudges her.

"Okay, mermaid. You see what you can do with these things. I just have to go in the bathroom — I'll be with you in a minute to help."

Seal closes the bathroom door, then, considering, cracks it open to keep an ear out for signals of help. Seal can hear rustling and the rubber squinch and pock of boots being slipped on, then off again.

"Rainy? If they're too big we can find some liners to put in them — look in the closet. Oh, wait a second, honey, I'll be out to help you." Seal has to open a new box of tampons. A period now, curse it. She doesn't believe it is that exactly, a curse, but it does appear at inopportune moments. Tears sting suddenly — another symptom, no doubt. It is so damned unnecessary, isn't it? Just a woman bodyclock, nest unfeathering itself over and over.

Seal, borrower of children, shifts uncomfortably, peeling back thin paper from the slick white tube with its sanitized cotton inhabitant, tidy little tail. Animal in a burrow, ought to have some use, some cunning crafty thing — instead of marking a death. Probably better have two, she thinks, judging from the deep curl of cramp wringing her womb.

The last time — wasn't it only three weeks ago? Just after Jacob called.

He'd arrived safely, he was full of his train travel, winding first down the snowy Mississippi for seventy miles. He sat behind "some old guys, in their twenties" and eavesdropped until they sent him away to the club car to fetch some Cokes.

"Jacob!" she reproved him.

"I bet they wanted to talk about girls without me listening. It was okay."

Jacob sounded so wise. He said the guys were cool; one was in the Peace Corps, the other was studying forestry.

"At first I was depressed."

"Because . . . ?" thinking he missed her, remembering his tears.

"Oh, they had great lives, you know, interesting . . . "

"Jacob, you too! You're so . . . " she was going to say young, so much ahead. But she didn't need to.

"Then they asked where I was going, so I thought I did interesting things, too, you know, travel. And I told them they should get Pepsi, not Coke. I told them to boycott Coke because of apartheid. So they were impressed, you know?"

Seal knew. Her body had sighed then, with relief for him. Her period started right after that. Now already another one.

The other room is still. "Rainy? Rainy!"

Seal's just been in the bathroom a couple of minutes. She'd heard the closet door opening, Rainy had understood about the liners — was it the closet door only? She'd heard no footsteps, but Rainy's small self did not make much noise. "Rainy?"

Not in the bedroom. Seal rushes into the living room; no Rainy. The front door is closed, but next to it, a thin new spray of snow spatters the mat. The turquoise coat — is it on the bed? She can see the end of the bed, not there, but she races back to check, stumbling on the throw rug in the hall, barking her shin on a stool that has never tripped her before. Should she telephone, and who? Maybe Rainy would head back toward the center. How could she, Seal, have been so careless? No time, maybe she can catch her if she runs. Seal grabs her own coat, slams out of the house. How could Rainy disappear so fast?

Footprints mark her and Rainy's path to the door; but another small pair crosses the front yard, and the prints are fast filling. A scrabble of packed indentations rings the igloo and leads into the covered opening by the forsythia bush. First Seal peers over the edge of the main bowl, dreading, but no human form is hunched inside, although the snow is marred. Rainy — or something — has been there. She could be hiding under the roofed entrance: Seal wastes valuable seconds crouching beside the bush, pushing her arms inside the igloo opening to sweep the ground where she cannot see, probing it insanely for child-sized humps, aching to hear her giggle, "Found me!" Rainy would not say that.

Any snowbank could conceal Rainy — not even her high pom-pom, skittering like a squirrel, would be visible above the white walls. Her throat constricted, Seal calls and calls, though her voice seems to thin and disappear into the snow. Breathing heavily, she lurches toward the street — aren't those footprints leading toward Franklin? The yard snow is many times trampled and covered, nothing clear except where a gust sweeps away new snow. No prints to the right, no person in sight, but toward busy Franklin, toward the center, the partly shoveled walk shows numbers of tracks.

Seal marches toward the street, craning her neck left and right, in case Rainy has cut through a yard. If Seal doesn't see her on Franklin, she'll call the police — no, not the police, yet. Rainy could be taken away from Jenna and it would be Seal's fault. She has to find her before . . . before something happens. Rainy could be only minutes ahead of her. Fresh footprints lead to the right on Franklin, a small and a large set . . . a large set. Seal breaks into a run.

A block and a half on, she sees them clearly, a woman leading a child, turning into Eddy's Cafe. Not Rainy. A taller child in a dark coat. Seal stops for breath. The hands wringing her insides seem to have reached upward, and her chest is tight. She coughs, to shake the feeling, and a whimper escapes. Maybe she'd better call the Center now, from Eddy's or the pay phone by the alley.

The alley.

The cat.

She backtracks, she's missed the footprints as she strained to see the human forms ahead; longer child's steps, running steps, lead toward the alley. Now there is no doubt. "Rainy!" she shouts, and hears a small cry on the wind.

Rainy is calling too. On tiptoe on an upended thirty-gallon galvanized garbage can, itself crowning an ice-bank, Rainy leans and calls into the dumpster. "Come on, come on . . . "

Intent on the cat crouching, baring its teeth, alive as an alleywise feline knows how to be, Rainy doesn't see Seal's arms stretched toward her until it's too late. The cat leaps, Rainy slips, kicking the galvanized can clanging down the ice-bank. Seal lunges, her arms gripping Rainy, and Seal's legs go separate ways. Her right knee hits ice, slides downward ridden like a surfboard by Rainy's red boots. Seal's head is buried in turquoise that fills her eyes like an ocean and muffles her scream. Seal's left leg slides under the legs of the dumpster, too quickly. Something snaps.

Her left side. Rainy rolls off, somehow, and stays beside her on all fours, shaking her head, puzzled. Seal can't locate the pain pulling her meanly from the soft dark, except that it's her left side, from her heel to her heart. She won't move, not even to straighten her right leg where she's leaning, half on it, half on the ice-hill. She wants to vomit, but it would hurt. Taking a deep breath would hurt.

She has to take soft breaths to fool the deep red animals inside, and fool Rainy. Don't worry her. "Phone, Rainy?" Seal licks her lips, trying to enunciate. Rainy's eyes are wild, showing too much white as she swivels them to the booth at the end of the alley. "9-1-1," Seal says softly, but without much hope. She has to give Rainy a quarter. "Pocket," she breathes, patting her right side carefully. Rainy rummages, but when she stands up with the change, shakes her head.

"Broke," she says.

Seal can't understand. Yes, her leg. That's not what Rainy means. The little girl trots to the booth, looking back to see that Seal's head follows her, and pantomimes an elaborate shrug, pointing to the broken seat, the instrument too high up. No good. "Rainy . . . " But Rainy disappears, hcr red legs flashing around the corner. It was too much for the child; Seal's failed again, frightened her.

Heavier snow finds its way into the alley, searching out Seal. It curls around her, touching her face with tentative insect cold. It wants her. She shifts, lifts both arms to pull her hood over the side of her face; but the pain hammers her chest and head, trying to knock her out. No way. She is more cunning then, closing her eyes to lull the pain, and slowly, slowly slides one hand up to fold the hood over her eyes.

But she speeds like a train through a tunnel of snow driving down the river, the world moving white, she moving through the world, all of them held up, she and Jacob and the two guys, and Rainy, too — wouldn't it be amazing?

If all the time Jacob and Rainy were safe, held in the basic good will of people, people who have nothing better to do than be kind.

She is, isn't she? You have to keep trying to think that way. You have to keep trying. She can't think clearly, but she feels her heart banging in its cage and she breathes to it, gentling it.

So she is not too surprised when the igloo comes to claim her, a rounded shape growing to take her in its arms, white and still, a perfect shelter. But he won't be still, though her eyes only half see him from her hooded cave: He is growing, coming closer. Big as a house in his white cook's apron, Eddy runs, Rainy close behind him. Eddy of Eddy's Cafe, her neighbor runs toward her, his jacket wide open to the wind. No sense at all. Amazing.

People of Color

I *shades*

I need a lot of space around me when I work. Sometimes it doesn't look like I'm working, I know, but still it has to be right.

I didn't always know that about myself. I'd chug around looking for company or inspiration or something. Sometimes I'd think I'd found it when I was in class and people would be around, but quiet, you know. The sound would ebb out as though someone opened a floor drain and, bloop, all the annoying machine and people noises, sniffles and scratches and whispers and worse would be gone. The prickle around my scalp and my fingers would stop; I'd shape the hair just right or the nose shadow and I'd look up and smile, but nobody was there to see.

So then I'd have the uneasy feeling that I'd insulted someone. I'd said something and made them go away, or I'd done something obnoxious like pick my nose without thinking, and they left. But I didn't remember. So I learned to shrug it off. I didn't used to shrug it off. I used to crumple up my work, or erase it; I didn't want it to be more important than my friends.

I don't know why people are so sensitive. Like last spring, Andy, this kid in my section. He'd get uptight about my comments, like about color, until he was used to me. Then he accepted that the brain was not necessarily connected to the mouth, especially when I was working. Actually, he was my roommate when we had three in the suite. See, we had this one tiny room that's like a dressing room, one dresser and a big mirror, and then two medium-sized rooms where we were supposed to put the bedroom and study room. Only there's not space enough for three beds in any of the rooms, so I won the dressing room, until Andy left. Andy said they put me in there because I made weird comments in my sleep and they'd stay awake all night trying to figure me out. Sure.

The reason he left was to go into the Marines. He is an African-American kid; he had my same name, Andrew. I guess the dorm thought they could keep better track of all the Andys if they were in the same room. I used to tell people we were really cousins, our sister-moms just happened to like the name Andy.

So I'm white. I mean I'm really white, it's some weird Irish throwback, what they call black Irish but the black is this blue-black hair, and skin like I don't know what. I'm basically tall and skinny like Dave, my gone paternal parent, instead of small-boned and round like my ma. But both of them are or were very white. Sometimes people ask if I have any blood. These Chicago winters I obtain some color walking to the subway in the wet wind from the lake, two chapped red spots high on my cheekbones. They add a little texture to an otherwise uninteresting face, color-wise. White as a plate, white as, uh, moonlight on a white chrysanthemum, ah so, master, I describe myself, I am specific without shade or relevance. Andy used to walk out of the room, you crazy, mothah, he said.

I have to learn about the space. I told my ma I needed a lot of space once, I was feeling frustrated but didn't mean it so heavy as it sounded. She just nodded once like she understood, but she tightened her lips. She thinks she's being cool. I wish she'd cut it out, treating me like I'm going to say something mean if she pushes me. I probably wouldn't now. I don't explode on contact.

I guess I used to explode. She reminds me of the time I took after Bull with a toy truck, Tonka, of course, well-made and steel. Bull's my brother, he acquired the name from me, when I was learning to talk; he's really Bill and he didn't like Bull, but the name stuck. Bull was ten and he used to tease me fiercely, putting my crayons up on the table when I'm drawing on the floor, or tugging at a corner of my paper little by little so I don't notice until I screw up. I was five and I started screaming, chasing him swinging the truck, and he was so surprised he sat down and didn't even duck.

Ma caught the truck before it caught Bull's ear. Then she sucked her hand and just looked at me; I was expecting her to slap me, or at least send me to my room, but she said, Billy, go on out and take the clothes down, would you? Don't tease him so.

I'm sure Bull was waiting to see me get it; he said, "Ma, he tried
to clobber me. I wasn't doing *anything* to him!"

I hitched myself under the table, just in case she made up her
mind to aim a swat at me anyway. I kept on drawing hard; I guess
it sounded as though I was whacking at the paper, but I was
drawing.

"Sweet baby," she says, but it was too quiet to be a sweet name,
"Why don't they have any heads?" She was crawling under the table,
pushing the chair out of the way to get at me. I sat up. Something
caught on the table, something on my head, my hat . . . why was
I wearing a hat in the house? Naturally she couldn't sit up; she
had to hunch down and twist her head to see me. I was crying
a little. "They gots heads." I used to say "gots" like everyone else
except my ma. She didn't correct me that time. She pointed at the
moustaches and noses and eyes, and she said, "I see what those
are but they're floating in air up above their shoulders. Don't you
want to put circles around them to define the heads?"

That was my features floating in air period, between five and
six, I guess. Ma still has them. She didn't say anything for a long
time under the table, so I went back to drawing.

"Sweetheart . . . "

"What!" My crayon forgot what it was doing.

"You were pretty mad at Billy."

I don't know why she brought it up again. Even back then, she
couldn't let things alone. Jeez, I was probably done being mad at
Billy, and now I was mad at her.

"No!" I meant I was done being mad and she was bothering me.

"Yes, yes you were."

"No, I'm not!" I started to cry again and she finally got hold
of me and I ducked my head; the thing kept getting caught. She
dragged me out; she talked a long time about being mad was okay,
but not hitting, but I thought she was acting like being mad wasn't
okay, at all.

II *Baby blue*

Man, I know some things. I know you can walk around on people's
hearts without taking a swing at them. Bull says yeah, now you
can use your mouth. I mean, this happened yesterday. I'm at my

station, see, and I remember saying something to a couple of the high school kids that are part of the class, early credit or something, and there's some laughing. I forget what it was. Most of the Chicago kids are pretty cool, they don't let stuff bother them; and anyway I was just getting this beautiful flare on the nose of Fred the Head. So I didn't look up. Next thing, the studio's empty and there's only this tick, tick from the pipes that comes on late when it's cold or the wind kicks up from the lake. It's cold, all right; you'd think this studio has been here since 1890 or when the Institute was just a school instead of a multi-million dollar monolith. The studio is huge, like a barn with no stalls except spaces corralled by easels and the rafters of canvases, and no warm cow or horse breath. Horrible thought, but it'd be warmer. Now the space is haunted only by drafts and a moaning under the skylight, which has turned cobalt blue, the midnight blue that makes me feel like singing Billie Holiday blues, if I could sing. The day seems to be heading toward dark, but I look at my watch, and I'm only twenty minutes late to my next class. Not so bad. They understand a little lateness around the Institute; some instructors are more understanding than others.

But I hate letting hours escape like that, it's like something has been knocked out of my day. Where's your head? Pay attention, she says. And at the same time, keep your eyes on the prize. How the hell can you do both things? She doesn't realize they're different. And Bull, what right did he have to say, you're gonna lose all your friends that way?

Bull used to have tons of friends, if you call them that, before. They still come around, but he doesn't have a lot of patience these days. Ma says he's different. Can't say as I see it, but then I'm not home except at vacation times. She thinks he used to be more easygoing than I am. "You're too intense, Andy!" she says. She should've seen him when he was loaded, that's probably why he cracked up that night, not because the cops beat him.

She always blamed the police. Bull's buddies gave her their biased point of view. They were just messing around at Lake and Hennepin, but the time frame was unfortunate, just after the demonstrations and the cops were edgy, even about white boys in clusters. Somebody said something, and this one cop grabbed Bull, just because he was the biggest, I guess. They took him in a building and did a drug search, b.c. — body cavities. Of course he was clean, beer was his drug of choice and he hadn't been drinking, yet. So they slap him around and tell him to get out. He took off, all right. Two hours later Ma has a call from the hospital; he'd cracked up his cycle, he has head injuries, but he'll recover. He had his helmet on; my brother's dumb but not that dumb. Still, he'd had a hematoma, a closed head injury. The result is, he has to learn a lot of shit he already knows.

For instance, that last month before I went to school he drove me crazy just being in the house with him. I like him, he's my brother, but the weird stuff gets to me. He understood; he tried to be quiet when I was working, but, like he'd start watering the plants. He'd come into the bathroom next to my room and pour one glass of water and walk down the steps to the first plant and then tromp up the stairs and run the water for thirty seconds. Full blast. You know how long it takes to fill an eight-ounce glass? Try it. Then stomp, stomp, down the steps and water the second plant. This goes on and on. We used to have a lot of plants. Ma never said anything, she just threw them out as they died limp and pale, fungal deaths. He's still intelligent and all, he hasn't lost it: it's that the controls are rusty. I finally ran to the bathroom door ready to scream at him. He's standing there scowling into the mirror like he can't stand the person inside.

I'm not going to show him the head I started last year, at least not for a while. The head is him in the mirror, only there's a crack through it and the right half is Andy, or sort of, Andy and me. It's the color of Andy; the left half is whiter, like me and Bull. Andy, like most U.S. African-Americans, isn't as black as I am white; he's probably more like cinnamon than pale brown, definitely not blue-black. Would I please come off it, he'd say, when I was Billie Holidaying to the blue, baby blue; or lighten up, won't you all please lighten up, and remember you're on a planet that's revolving and evolving at, I forget. Whenever I croon, Andy groans; but he was interested in spite of himself when he saw me mixing to match his skin. He'd put his arm next to the palette and say, hell, you never get it, Jack — and I'd say, I'm not doing cosmetics for you, Henry, I gotta put some of this rich sick green under your eyes, see?

God, that was a good head. Never had the nose right, though, or the eyes; Bill's are blue, and Andy's — Andy had too many colors.

III *Cinnamon*

No, cinnamon was more like Chua Ma Johnson. Funny I never tried to paint her. Not that I don't want to, someday, but the space isn't there to put her in. She's there, relatively perfect; I'm talking about color and shape, and whatever I'd paint, it would be something else. Maybe that's okay, but later, not now. Or maybe what happened is that when she was around I felt like touching her instead of the paint.

She smells like cinnamon, too. But I wouldn't know how to color her; she changes. She's painted with light, like a hologram of a peach under a halogen lamp when you have the angle right, just before the cinnamon comes in.

She's Vietnamese and Swedish, poor kid. We sort of connected at the therapist's group because I told her I never knew my dad either. She's a blend, like a fine wine, my cinnamon wine I called her. She pushed me away when I said stuff like that, but probably because I was saying it with my nose in her neck and it's difficult to articulate properly when your nostril is hung up in a collar button.

She's proud to know her name. She was in St. Paul because she figured the Twin Cities were good places to look for a father named Johnson.

"So how do you even know the name is right?" She must have realized there were lots of Johnsons. "He could lie."

She didn't like that. She sat up straight on my bed, which was not as erotic as it sounds, most of my furniture having shifted to Chicago, and we being perched on the remnants of my carefree summer quarters at Ma's. This was the last chance romantic parting until Christmas, and it wasn't going well.

"My mother told me, before she died, she said he was a soldier and she and he were very close. I could tell she loved him. She always carried his picture and now I carry it."

She showed it to me for the umpteenth time. He still looked like half the rotcee guys in my old high school, long head, blond, skinny with padded uniform shoulders. He'd look older now, of course.

I never knew what to say. I thought she was really brave coming here on the Unaccompanied Minors program, not knowing what kind of family she'd be hooked up with.

"I'm very strong."

"Good. Let's arm wrestle." My arm next to her calf, I stroked it, pretending I thought it was her arm. "Sweet wrist you have, little bone, little round . . . ouch!" She rapped my head with her knuckle.

"I don't mean arm-strong. I mean my head, my thoughts, you understand?"

I smiled innocently at her. "Headstrong?"

She frowned. Her frown made me think of tiger lilies. "Strong in my desire. No, stop cutting up, Andy! In my will, you know?"

"Willful."

"I suppose. I will find him positively."

I had almost convinced her how strong and wonderful and above all lovely she was when a timid, then a firm knock interrupted us. Even though this was my inviolate bedroom, the house was lacking in certain privacies.

Ma offered to make up the guest bed for Chua if she was planning to stay over, otherwise I'd best drive her home, as it was three in the morning and we had to start for Chicago early. I could tell she was keeping cool for Chua's sake but no way in hell would she let Chua sleep over unless she called her foster mother, and she didn't have the hots for calling anybody's mother at three A.M.

That was the last time we saw each other. Ma wrote that Chua was moving; then around Thanksgiving, I received a letter from Chua in California asking me to send her Chicago and suburbs phone numbers for Johnson. After I was done banging my head against the mailbox, I did xerox eleven pages of Johnsons, mentioning in my note that most likely the bulk of them in Chicago were not Swedes. And if she was ever in Chicago she could dial her little fingers blue from my place. So far she hasn't written back.

Well, Andy wasn't as pretty as Chua, but he did have his good points. I think we used to like each other. We spent time, you know? So when we were out together, I'd say we were cousins and people would look at me like they don't know what's polite. That's what I liked about saying it. But one time Andy got pissed right in front of some girls I was putting on, and he said to never do that again. I said, "Don't you like being my cousin, man?" And he said, "Man, I don't even like being your *brother,* you keep messing with my race, racist!" The girls faded — I followed Andy home with my head down, thinking he could at least look back and note my contrite unmilitary bearing, but he never did.

Still, he said, brother.

I don't remember exactly how I came to know him. Or if. You know how you do in a new school, new town. We were in the same dorm, we'd see each other in different classes that first week and sit near each other — everything else was so strange. Our dorm was a few miles from the Institute. It wasn't like regular college campuses where you're in a small town and you see everybody swinging through the green lawns and the elm petals are dripping on them, then they go to have a Coke in the Union. So the freshpeople dorm kids were like the old neighborhood, vaguely familiar to each other those first weeks. And we'd all tromp out together at night and catch the El together, going north. Andy and I talked about renting an apartment this year with Rick. Only now it's just me and Rick.

I don't know why the hell he went. Well, I do, it was before this Gulf stuff, and he'd only had money for one semester, and the Marines said they'd make good use of his talent.

I asked what talent was that, flame-throwing, because he was into welding found objects first semester. At the time, I was chipping dinner off the bottom of the ricaroni pan, so I said, what the hell is this, anyway, new technique for sculpture, charred glue? Cleanup of cooking disaster was supposed to be the cook's job, so I guess I sounded a tad acerbic. But he took it well, as I remember; he said, No shit, they gonna make me a cook for sure, Andy babes. And I'm gonna mail you a box of cookies every week! Not like your mama!

You've got to understand about my mom. She can cook; but she sends us sugarless health cookies, and puts chocolate chips in them. Not carob, the real poison. I'm not fond of them, I never ate that health stuff all my life, so I guess she's getting even: bran cereal and oat bran and wheat germ and nuts. I do eat them, no choice if you're a starving artist and not much better a cook than Andy Two. Andy Two, though, used to crumble them up at breakfast and pop the chocolate chips on the side. He put milk and sugar on the crumbs, says it isn't half bad and it's 3.99 a box for the same stuff at Kroger's.

Anyway, Mom had dinner with us at Wong's one day last spring when Andy was getting ready to go. This restaurant's in our neighborhood, Greek/Italian, run by a Chinese family. We couldn't afford it, but Mom was charmed and dragged us along.

So she points her forkful of saganaki at Andy and says, "Don't go. Please," she says, "you can't know what it's like, what you'll have to think." Remember this is the spring *before* our buddy Saddam became criminally Hussein, but she has this particular point of view. Andy starts talking history, Korea, and the way the UN messed that up. Ma kept shaking her head, so he talked about the promises the Marines made.

He didn't mention money, though, so Ma didn't understand. She glared at him. "Teach you," she says, "they teach killing! That's not what you boys are about." Andy shut down. His face turned bland and soft and he didn't even hear the tears in her throat when she said, "you're about creating!"

IV *Blood*

Tonight on the phone she tells me about the protest at the St. Paul Marine Recruiters' office. She said she thought about Andy. The staff sergeant was African-American, so her friend says, "It's your people in the Persian Gulf." I guess the sergeant was ticked off because he says, "My people are all kinds of people." My mom thought that was cool. So what's he supposed to think about all these white ladies, mostly ladies, coming in and spilling blood all over his letterhead, talking about his people.

I just had a letter from Andy, so I read her some parts of it.

You were right about one thing — I don't get a lot of painting time except for personnel carriers. But Andy One, there's a lot of the brothers here, big beautiful ones with green faces like you want to paint, ain't you jealous? & they groove on my drawings. I have a new technik with grit and motor pool paint. Grit's in everything especially teeth so I might as well use it. Everybody in my quarters is a person of some kinda color, "self selected," the Sarge says, ain't that nice? & tell your mama we did learn those pretty marching songs from Nam like she said, "rape the town & kill the people, that's the stuff we like to do" — it's a hellhole allright, but there's color around me — I have a crazy mother-brother almost crazy as

you; he mouths off to the Sarge, says to him if you white boys don't
get to kill somebody soon, you gonna kill somebody.

She was quiet for at least thirty seconds. Then she told me about
this black northside group protesting police violence, they were
meeting with the militants to maybe combine their marches.

"Hey, that's interesting," I said.

"Really, maybe they can get across some messages about
militarism and racism."

"Ism-ism." My ear was becoming numb, and she knew politics
wasn't my bag. She changed the subject and told me about pick-
ing up the Marine's sword, displayed in the window. She was
laughing so I couldn't hear anything but little wheezes. I waited,
I can be patient when it's not my phone bill.

"I drew it out of its scabbard and I said, WHAT is this thing?
and I'm waving it around so the people looking in through the
plate glass window can see. The recruiters were calm; they just
held on to their desks, but you should have seen the cop who was
waiting to arrest us. He was apoplectic! He says, lady, we'll all be
happier if you'd put that thing away. I said, How do you USE this
heavy thing?" She took a breath. "The sergeant said it was
ceremonial. It was just in the window for DISPLAY!"

"Real Freudian. So did you put it away, or are you charged with
sword mauling?"

"Oh sure. No, I'm charged with criminal damage. Dripping on
the desk, from my own vial."

I asked what she thought would happen to her, but she didn't
know yet. I was a bit curious to know if someone would be around
at Christmas break — I told her I could always heat up some beans,
see my friends.

But I couldn't hear any guilt; most likely she was rolling her eyes
toward heaven. "Andy, I want to ask you something."

I knew what was coming.

"Did you send in your request yet?"

She meant the C.O. request. I hadn't. I wasn't going to, at least
not now. I especially didn't want to be pressured about it.

"I talked to this guy, a counselor," I said. That was sort of true.
He spoke at a teach-in about letters of support to gather, and
worksheets to figure out your particular religious objections to war

and all kinds of bureaucratic stuff that probably wouldn't mean shit to a draft board. "He said a draft was unlikely at this point," I said aloud.

"Really? But Andy, you're going to be twenty the day before the deadline and the twenty-year-olds are the first ones called, I heard that much."

"The January fifteen deadline is just a political ploy, ma. Bushy says there won't be any draft, too."

"Andy!" she practically shrieked.

"Yeah, I know, who do I believe, my president or my mother. Hmm."

"Please do it." I didn't like the tone I heard, like she was already beaten, giving up on me.

"Listen," I said, "Can we talk about it Christmas?" I mean, I was prepared to talk about all of it, maybe not at that moment, but I'd been working on it, the service question. There were things I wanted to know. My father *was* a Marine.

"The sooner you build your file . . . "

I cut her off. "I just have to know some things first; maybe you can't tell me everything, but I need to be clear about this!" I was as surprised as she was at the harshness in my voice.

"Andy, what are you talking about?"

So maybe it was time. "I want to know exactly why Dave, why my dad left that day? I mean, you don't have to tell me now, but I want to know so I can . . . " I couldn't finish the sentence.

I heard her breath draw in. And her voice was harder when it came on. "I wish you'd waited until we were together. But I guess it's relevant now, isn't it?"

I nodded, which was ridiculous, but she apparently heard my nod.

"You talked about Dav — your father — with Dr. Bradley?"

"Sure. But not about that day. I couldn't remember much."

"Oh, Andy, you were so small. What can you remember?"

I talked slowly, trying to call up the picture. "That day you stopped me from clobbering Bull with the truck . . . "

"That's not right. That was a week later. He was gone. David was dead by then."

"Let me finish. I had stuff on my head. It kept getting caught on the table — gauze, I had a bandage on my head."

I could hear her crying while I was bringing the words out, but quietly.

Her voice was thick when she came on again, but I could hear her fine. "He was leaving. He wanted to run away because he couldn't stop the noise, he said, he couldn't hear anything else . . . "

"You mean Bull and me?" I'd always thought so, that it was our fault, partly, even when Bradley explained that kids do think that way, and that it's not necessarily up to us what happens with parents.

"No. Andy, no. Sometimes when you cried he was upset and he'd have to go out, but mostly the noise he meant was at night, the guns and the screams in his mind. Nightmares. Then sometimes he had them when he was awake, too, more and more. He started screaming again, just as he was leaving. All I wanted to do was to stop him, stop the hysteria."

I was confused. "Who did it?"

"What? Who did what? I mean, I hit him, I wanted to stop him. Several times. And then you . . . " she started crying again.

"Ma, who did it, whose fault was it?"

"You were screaming at him, both of you were screaming. I wanted you to get away from him, to go in the other room, I swatted you, too. I'm not sure of the whole scene, I was half crazy too . . . "

"*He* threw me, didn't he? He pushed me into the wall, the corner of it, I remember his hand then I couldn't see . . . "

"Andy. I think that part was an accident, really — maybe he was trying to get you away too. Anyway, that's what did it. He saw the blood. He touched you, really so softly . . . and then he walked out the door."

"While I was bleeding? Did he even know what he was doing?"

"I don't know. I was frantic, I couldn't find the keys at first, I put a washcloth on your forehead; I didn't see which way he went. All I cared about was that he didn't take the car. It wasn't as bad as it looked, a head cut *bleeds,* they told me. You were fine."

"Fine." I was sitting on the floor. "I think I'll go sit under the table awhile." I laughed, weakly, as they say. I really did feel more or less fine, but . . . "Why didn't you tell me all this?"

"I guess I thought you remembered more . . . like it was imprinted. You were so solemn and good in the car, holding that rag to your head . . . I remember I said, I'm sorry, I'm sorry, and you said, 'I know it.' Andy. The fault thing. It's everybody's fault, not just his. Do you understand? I hit you, maybe I would have gone on hitting you. But then I didn't go on."

"Right on. Go and sin no more." Maybe I sounded too ironic. I like irony. Everybody's fault — the war's fault? I don't know. But I ended up the conversation with, "love you too," so she'll be okay.

In the last part of Andy's letter, after "we know this ain't our war . . . but they have to put us somewhere, and we're together. We get some compensation . . . " he says, "Andy don't come."

I know he's not trying to hurt my feelings. I know what he means. But I might still go, they might need troops there for a long time. I won't fight the draft, if it comes. Or maybe I will, like my mom, maybe I'll decide to go to jail; I don't know, it's another option. All I know is I'm not going to just walk away.

The Catch

It's only sex, after all, that high thrilling pipe from the pine trees and from the wetland barely released from its winter lock. The big-throated tree frogs already insist, an unending heartache cry, one voice then more, overlapping one another, crying: we want, we want, you, you, you.

The sound awes the straggling group of white people, who pick their way gingerly through the singing trees, their own voices hushed. They are come to witness, not this amphibian choir, but the St. Croix Band spearfishers as the fishers take their harvest of walleye in spawn.

Besides these — the fishers, the frogs, and the non-native supporters and native people — two larger groups crowd the clearing near a public boat landing on Star Lake. The Enemy, for reasons having to do with the local economy, or ignorance, or excitement, means to stop the tribe from spearing. The Law, sheriffs and state troopers ranged beside the lake in relaxed rows, is here to generally keep an eye out.

Nancy stumbles through the brush with the first group, the supporters, who are a little frightened by the dark surround-sound of the frogs. Not only the unseen shrill insistence in the pines, but the drum speaks now, rumbling in an unfamiliar cadence that Nancy is trying to think is encouragement.

Catcalls of the opposition are somehow less ominous to her. She can see the Enemy: they carry signs like "Save a walleye/spear an Indian" and "Welfare Warriors." They seem hearty and high-spirited, with an edge of laughter in the face of seamy adventure. Clusters of witnesses try to shush the sign carriers so that the drum and the drummers — four young men, but like the frogs they sound like more — can have their full power for the fishers.

Nancy breathes easy in the clear challenge; she takes her station near the drum, which is the center of action, or at least noisy attention now that the spearers are launched. The drum is nestled up against a snow fence that separates the police and the launch site from the public. Nancy is part of a buffer zone to absorb the jeers and fake warwhoops. Because of her, she thinks, fewer taunts and no rocks can graze the ears of the harvesters out on the black lake.

Curt Peterson is a member of the opposition, but he's a fisherman himself and has a personal stake in the controversy. If all goes well, he'll be a landowner near this lake. Like Nancy, though he doesn't know her yet, he's originally from Minneapolis. He's come to Star Prairie to live with clean snow. Curt believes the Minneapolis incinerator, thrust into the city near its downtown heart, maybe in its left lung, put the finishing gray film on the winters. If you had to put up with ice and cold half the year, it could at least be scenic.

Star Prairie is still scenic, a town small and dim enough that on such cloudless nights in spring you can sit on the clearcut side of a hill rising from Star Lake and see whole meadows of stars. Curt's wife Darlene had agreed readily to the move, even pregnant with Patricia, called Peanut. Curt's unemployment checks from the Ford plant layoff carried them while he worked his way into small repairs and locksmithing. Curt has good hands. They are efficient on small machinery, sensitive to the tremulous changes in tumblers inside jammed locks and, so Darlene says, sensitive on her, too. Two years after the move, however, business isn't great, because most of his new neighbors manage to fix their own small engines and, so far, locks aren't the commodity they are in the Cities.

But he considers himself a Star Prairian for the future; Star Lake spawns fish for his own little girl, who on some July day will lean over the placid water, breathing lightly to entice the red-and-white bobber to dip for certain. It will not be her impatient chubby hands shaking the pole, making the bobber tremble by accident — this time it will be a real sunny, a sunfish with a gold-red belly like Peanut's sunsuit that day she leaned over the strut in the canoe to watch the water and Darlene grabbed her and paddled her little bottom so fast, never, never stand up in a boat! As though the paddling didn't shake the canoe worse, and shook Peanut's confidence, too. Curt would see that she was safe. He'd make her wear a lifejacket, and they'd never go out after twilight, when the summer sunnies bit.

Nancy stares at Curt, at the momentary anguish then the slow smile that sweetens his drawn Scandinavian-morose features. What is he thinking of, she wonders, some plan of action these young guys have? Nancy and Curt are separated by politics and intentions but by only a few feet of grass. Nearby, the drum begins a quiet grumbling that they both suspect will soon drive at their ears.

Curt's eyes are on one of the Indian drummers, whose lips are pulled back stiff, almost in a sneer, until his cheeks shiver like the squalls that riff the lake's dead calm in summer. The Indian's animal-skin drumstick head picks up speed in synchrony with the three others stroking the taut skin. Curt's breath escapes in a "pah!" of admiration, and his eye finally catches Nancy's.

"What's so interesting, lady?" Curt backs off a step and leans on his Welfare Warrior sign.

Nancy shrugs and turns to the drummers. She doesn't need the hassle, but she had been staring — which was rude — out of interest in the mind behind the pleasant face, the mind that could think to carry such a sign. Of course, he hadn't invented it; the slogan was blatant on bumper stickers on back roads and in back hallways leading to rest rooms in highway cafes.

On the road from St. Paul, Nancy had been in such a place, not a bar but having the atmosphere of a bar, where she felt noticed by the mumbling tables of men in feed hats, as she searched out the women's room. The waitress finally pointed her to the back hall, where Nancy had just been, and had seen the offensive sign, along with a sign for "Gentlemen." "That's it, honey. There's only the one."

And why not? Nancy chided herself; the cafe was a small place, it conserved resources. A condom machine looming over the toilet looked newly installed, but was no longer a clue to the gender orientation of the john. She'd seen the machines in women's rooms before. The names were softened now, extending the jock appeal of Magnum and Trojan; Sheik Elite and CarEss suggested security and sophistication. They were, apparently, colored and textured, too, to signify that safe didn't have to be boring.

The train of thought was not helpful to her queasy stomach, the reason she'd needed the rest room in the first place. Riding three in the back seat of a Honda on county roads in pothole season and sharing tuna sandwiches didn't do much for her equanimity, let alone her digestion. In the car, her group had seriously discussed the correctness of tuna; no one knew whether Chicken of the Sea was boycotted, or if the dolphin-endangering fishing methods had changed. They resolved to research the issue once they were back on home territory. For tonight, Nancy, who had made the sandwiches and was annoyed at this digression, reminded everyone that they were responsible anyway for keeping their strength up.

"Life's little ambiguities," she told them.

Like being here. She had been invited to put her money where her mouth was, a crude metaphor her ex-husband Lee employed to scoff at her interest in indigenous studies. She wanted to tell her third-grade students about real Indians, slaughtered five hundred years ago and oppressed by society today. But since Lee had moved to Minoqua with his bimbette Lisa, he thought he knew more about Indians than Nancy did.

"You ought to experience the tension up here, Nancy, before you start talking about white oppression."

She'd only called him to ask him to return her Columbus books. Her name was neatly printed on the flyleaves on her own books and her property should have been respected. Not that Lee had got away with much else, after he and Lisa took from her what mattered.

"I have adequate tension in my life, thanks," she reminded him. Even with the house, and the newer car, the dregs of a fourteen-year marriage were hard to live on.

"I'm only making a suggestion, babe. Go to a landing. Talk to people. Put your money where your mouth is."

"Save your diminuitives for Lisette, why don't you? All I want is my books."

"My what?"

But on cool-headed consideration, after she'd closed the phone over his meandering excuses, Nancy thought Lee's idea of going to observe the spearfishing was a good idea. She could experience first-hand any racism, and hear the real issues.

She had prepared. She attended a treaty rights conference on Franklin Avenue, in a neighborhood she usually avoided, and she endured the eye-stinging envelopment of tobacco and some very long speeches. She wrote definitions in a spiral-bound book: "reserved" were the rights of the Ojibway in "ceded" territories, lands turned over by treaties in 1837 and 1842. Treaties were international, not state law. Laws were complicated, but somehow a federal judge managed to rule that the law that could feed a tribal band really was a law and should be obeyed. Facts and figures followed.

Nancy's busy pen could scarcely keep up, but she wrote that Indians didn't harvest most of the fish caught; sport fishers took ninety percent (in rounded numbers, as the serious young man with the ponytail pointed out). Indians didn't seek the egg-filled females. There were upper limits on size and ninety percent of the take was the smaller male. "One for our side," Nancy whispered to her neighbor, but the Indian woman shushed her, and Nancy lost track of the numbers.

She feels, nevertheless, that she is primed with essential background and is free to enjoy righteous spirit of the drum, pumping its heartbeat onto the cold lake. In a minute she will take her courage in hand to dialog, nonviolently, with the opposition.

Curt, still eyeing the back of Nancy's head and remembering the frosty sea-colored eyes below blond bangs a little too long, knows what the issues are for him. The Indians have their own land to live on, whereas he will have to save who knows how many years for what he wants. And now they can fish any time any place they want to. He thinks it's favoritism.

Sea-colored is exactly what Curt thinks of Nancy's eyes because, although he isn't given to poetic description, even around women, and has not in his life seen an ocean, he is impressed by the bread commercial on television where a man in hip boots stands insanely amid the turbulent waves of Hudson Bay, stupidly shouting praises of bread, while the cold gray-green waves churn around him. Those are her eyes. The bangs nearly in them and the hair sticking out in back like a tail, swishing a bit with the drum, are a warm sand color.

"Hey, Sandy!"

The swatch of hair stills, but she doesn't turn around. Not Sandy, then, he thinks . . .

Then suddenly Curt is on television himself. The area around the drum lights up like a stage; drummers' shadows elongate into the police lines and the pines beyond them, shadows crazily climbing the tree trunks. A camera sneaks up behind Curt, poking its snout over his shoulder for a better view. Now the camera sweeps the drummers and crowd, and backs off to take a square look at Curt and his sign as a lady with a microphone approaches him. The mike is thrust under his nose like smelling salts. It smells of sweaty rubber.

Curt, surprised, is eloquent. "Racism doesn't have anything to do with why I'm here," he says. "The races have to work together, we have to conserve our resources for the future, like my little daughter."

The television lady is sympathetic. "How old is your daughter?"

"Only two and a half, but she already likes to fish." This is an exaggeration, so Curt seizes the opportunity to expound.

"That's what my sign 'Welfare Warriors' means — there's no bravery in taking away from one group of people to give to another, is there? Equal rights, that's what America should be about." But the lady is moving off to another sign holder.

At least now Curt has the sandy girl's attention; he is a celebrity, he has a message.

"Equal rights, you were saying," Nancy nods vigorously; she is going to make a point, going to skewer him where he stands on the matted slick ground; "What are *you* going to give back?"

She means, originally, for always. Isn't he the male of the species, the taker? She means he represents the plow that tore the webbing of the land, the axe that made white scars on the body where green timber stood. She means, though she can sputter only part of her insight, that they should give it back, give back the walleye (polluted anyway) for which white fat tourists probe the deeps all sweaty summer with electric machines.

She also means, though she says nothing of this, that the takers have robbed her, too, in the person of her ex-husband Lee, who talked the lawyers out of Nancy's cherry loveseat; she capitulated, signing it over to him, helping him load it into their van, though only after she scratched a hidden curse on its underside.

"Hey, hey," Curt backs up, spreading his mittened hands to demonstrate, no weapons here. "What do *I* have? I'm barely making it myself."

Nancy shakes her head, ashamed of her emotion. If she's going to dialog, she must use her reason. "Sorry, I was carried away. Your statement made me think."

"Statement?"

Nancy takes Curt's arm and nods toward the edge of their cluster of people, to guide him away from the drum's noise. He follows her slowly. She isn't as pretty as her hair, now that she looks so stern and preachy.

"We can talk now," she declares. "Your statement to the press. You raised an interesting point."

"Glad to hear it," he says, confused.

"Is your argument that there aren't enough fish for everybody?" She is going to quote statistics that white anglers take more fish than spearfishers, but he isn't prepared to hear.

"I fished here two years," he says angrily. "Two years ago I took my limit almost every day. Last year the fish were smaller, so the DNR restocked. You know how many years it takes to get big fish?"

She doesn't.

"You know what my bag limit is next year?" He moves closer; her eyes widen and take on some sea life again. She doesn't know what his bag limit is.

"Two. Two little fish at a time. Not enough for three people to eat."

She tries to change direction, "You're married . . . you have a little girl."

He nods, still grim, still in her face. "Curt Peterson." But he doesn't extend a hand. They are enemies.

The drum stops, and in the sudden silence Nancy's words come out too loudly, portentous. "Nancy Sunstrom, I mean, Smith," she stutters, "Nancy Smith," not even remembering her new-old name in a stressful situation, having to return to plain maidenly Smith, another privilege lifted away along with "Mrs." and its perquisites. "I'm a teacher, in St. Paul," she adds.

"Ms. Smith, the schoolteacher," Curt grins. He likes her now well enough to tease, "What else don't you know about fishing?"

"I used to fish! Lee's family has a cabin near Hayward, and we . . . " She stops. This is beside the point. "Now I don't," she shrugs.

"So what are you doing here? What's your stake?"

Her stake? Last night she dreamed, a recurrence of a nightmare she'd had as a child, that her own family's vacation lake had drained out, the clear water disappearing as though someone had pulled a plug. A highway, pinned in place by surveyors' stakes, spilled through red mud; she remembers the bare ground was red, like an open wound, and the forest ended.

"I'm a witness," she says irritably. "I'm helping to keep the peace."

Curt laughs. "The boys in blue will do that." He gestures to the police, who have peeled back from their heavy presence near the fence and stand talking among themselves near the shore. Many have apparently left. A DNR truck backs up to the dock, preparing to count and size the catch when it comes in. A motor on the water coughs, clears its throat, and pours out into a steady whine; spearers are moving to another bay — successful? Some tension has lifted.

What is she doing here? Abruptly, Nancy sits down, puts her head between her knees. The queasiness is back; her ears ring loud enough to shut out the one drummer playing around testing the drum, an aimless muttering. If she can't stop shivering, she'll throw up. She worries that her period is going to start; the witness trainer advised them not to come if that was the case. The power of women at menses might detract from the spearing. Nancy would be responsible.

A sentence from the Indian Fish and Wildlife Commission booklet jumps into her mind: "On some lakes, tribes and sportsmen work side by side to strip the females of their eggs." It means only that they can cooperate, Indians and others — not anything sinister. But Nancy is dizzy, thinking about the mama fish, less than ten percent of course, a mistake, but still her belly is opened, busy fingers, pale and sun-reddened and darker, quickly strip the eggs, to restock the empty waters. . . .

"Nancy! Nancy, are you okay?" An arm braces her back, and a gloved hand tips her chin to hold something warm to her lips.

"Quit it!" she jerks her head away. "I just have to sit down —
stomachache."

Curt sits beside her, offering a flask. "It's just coffee and a little
brandy. It might help."

More brandy than coffee, she thinks, but it's warm, hot even,
going down, and seems to steady her.

"You're still shivering," Curt informs her. "Come on, we can wait
and warm up in my car. They'll be in soon. We can talk more."

At the moment, Nancy thinks, her interest in dialoging is nil,
but being warm sounds attractive, even necessary. A nasty ice-pellet
wind shifts up from the lake; they are not the only couple heading
toward the road. Nancy's group, though, is staunchly huddled on
the shore gazing outward, waiting, she guesses, for the last fishy
gasp.

Curt's Toyota is half-hidden by a stand of pines overlooking the
lake, but she'll be able to see if the others leave; all the cars will
begin leaving. Curt's car gleams warmly, a little red beacon perched
on a ledge, only a sapling or two between it and the water.

"Is this safe?" Nancy wants to know. The ground is only half-
frozen, spongy and stiff by turns, a spiderweb glaze of ice over black
pools in the deeply rutted road.

"I park here all the time. You have to back out, but it's okay.
You climb in back, I'll run the motor a minute," he promises, and
does so as Nancy bundles herself in a wool blanket on the back seat.

The vibrations are soothing, as is the brandy, and she kicks her
boots off, tucking her feet up under her thighs. She is wrong to
suspect him.

Then he shuts off the motor and in a moment cleverly folds his
body over the folded down passenger seat. He arrives nearly in
her lap. The car rocks with the sudden movement, but settles again.

"Curt, I'm not really up for this, I could be sick," she whines.
Nancy is determined to be direct.

So is Curt. "Me either, I couldn't, it's too cold. So move over."

Nancy sighs, and welcomes him into the blanket; they can take
the comfort of wrangling children, too tired to continue the
struggle. "Pass the coffee."

A third swallow unaccountably cures Nancy's stomachache. She
smiles at Curt, "I'm a rotten witness," gesturing toward the dwindling

crowd, "I'm supposed to be with them, putting their bodies on the line, braving the cold."

"Your body is fine where it is." His companionable arm reaches around her, and they listen a moment to the distant drum, which has awakened, and the high-pitched song of the young men, sounding happier now.

"So, how was the car trip up here?" Curt asks.

"The trip." She doesn't want to think about the bumpy road, or the condom cafe. "Oh," she remembers, "It seemed like spring, finally." She tells him parts of the drive, how a late afternoon kindliness lay on the dips and shallows of farmland, with a tinge of green that hadn't reached the shade of the woods. Everything seemed gold-edged at that time of day, the high clouds, the open ponds, the sharp old-growth cattails — a mellow scene, with mallards rising at the appropriate moment. Then she sees again the Strips, the commercial belt between country and mid-sized towns, the schlocky sameness of franchise and pavement — McDonald's, Midas, Econowash, Burger King, Gulf. Super-America, MidAmerica, Southtown Buick, Southtown mall: Wallmart or K-Mart, Hallmark, Hardee, empty lot, Will Subdivide, empty flashing plate glass, For Rent. Pizza Hut, Taco Bell, Long John Silver selling cod and clam, ocean come to the woods. The plastic, useful, serviceable Strip underpinned the towns, she thinks, like a garter belt over the broad flanks of the land.

"Don't cry," he says, his hand somehow on her flank, underneath her long underwear, where the car seat trembles and tips, so she has to put her hand on the floor for balance, and feels the floor move, sickeningly.

The drum, with the vagaries of sound carried on gusts of wind and curves of the path winding around brush and pines toward them, has been with them all this time, has in fact slowly enveloped them. The muffled beating surrounds them, vibrating against the metal and their ears as though they're inside it.

Bodies slide against the doors and windows — Indians' heads appear, light from their foreheads and eyeglasses glittering through the fogged glass, staring hilariously at Nancy and Curt as though they are trapped fish in an aquarium. The car lurches, and her head knocks against the window.

They are going to push the car into the lake, Nancy knows. What has she done, to go out this way, smelling of brandy and dead tuna? It will be a mistake, they can't tell she's on their side, a gross irony. All she can think is, broken treaties, broken promises. She grabs Curt's hand; it's gone cold on her thigh, and his face is white, staring at the lake. Trees sweep slowly around them, as the tires scrape frozen mud and gravel.

Then there is no scraping; they seem to be airborne, like flying dreams where she is only inches above the ground, drifting by mind control. Except that she is not in control here, neither of them is in control; they are captured.

Laughter surrounds the red cocoon and its unhappy, tainted contents as Curt and Nancy realize they are not to be sacrificed after all, but pulled back from the edge. Someone in the celebratory dance that followed the drum, beating heat back into the blood of the fishers and supporters, that wove through the clearing and up the hill, to the cars, someone has taken note of their danger. They are treated well, for spoils. On the arms of the victors, the small catch is lifted, danced from the mud and deposited gently, in the middle of the road toward home.

Relatives

S hut up, Peanut," Darlene says, but nicely, putting a mother's warm mouth stretch into it. Meaning, this little girl has been clapping "Jingle Bells" for an hour as they drove, and it's early May. Here at Bonnie's Viands in the mall, it nowise matches the funky wail of the shopping center's fashion rock muzak. The backbeat does have a little of Peanut's driving monotony, boompadaba, boompada. That reminds her, that left rear tire must have had a stone in it, the roads from home aren't that evenly rough. Peanut's croon had had a steady waver that wasn't her own. She'll have to tell Curt. Darlene clicks her tongue, impatient at herself. As if she's going back to Curt!

They left Curt and Star Prairie for good this time, that's the truth of it. Darlene just has to shut down that part of her brain that refers certain mechanical questions and a multitude of sensory experiences to Curt. Such mental conversations used to fill long stretches of every day. Who did she think of when she noticed small events, when Curt was out mowing or down at the shop? For instance: the musical creak, high note low note, just at the head of the stairs up from their landlady's, and only if you stepped a certain way. Or the 3-D effect Darlene gave to the maple leaf shadows on the wall, if she pulled the sheers across the window; Peanut's concentration at turning a page of her Pooh book; a nailhead pooching out, a pimply shadow on the sheetrock, near the ceiling.

Curt praised her for that last; he said she was the greatest noticer, especially if it meant something had to be fixed. Nell, their landlady, had been in a hurry getting the apartment ready for them. You were supposed to tap in the nails a smidgen, and smooth the plaster-mud over the indentations. Not all the nails were properly plastered over.

The waitress behind the gleaming glass counter holds up a coffee pot. Refill? Darlene and Peanut are the only customers at the tables in front of Bonnie's Viands, which offers veggie health food and scrumptious-looking whipped cream and chocolate constructions. Darlene holds out her glass mug and Peanut mimics her, as she does so well, cupping in her fat little hands her Tommy Tippee, the supposedly unspillable cup with the weighted round bottom. The cup had been Darlene's when she was a baby, a plastic heirloom that spilled plenty but never managed to break.

"Me, me, me, me," Peanut chants.

"Would your daughter like some juice?" the waitress asks politely. The waitress' fluffy hair is piled back in a highsprayed ponytail and she is all skinny legs in a black skimpy skirt. Darlene has a better shape, or would have again. Better, anyway, on top, where she is filled out well from the new pregnancy, but her womb was only just pushing at her skirt buttons, so she still was slender below. She shouldn't be having so much trouble landing a job.

"Daughter? We're just buddies up for some shopping and a good time, right, honey?"

Peanut doesn't know what she's talking about but giggles and repeats, "Me!"

"Bring her something blue, she won't know the difference. Blue juice is her favorite."

Peanut looks doubtfully at the raspberry-grape bottle when it comes, but as soon as Darlene pours it into Tommy Tippee, she sucks contentedly at the spout. The drink costs a dollar seventy-nine, so Darlene fishes in her fanny pack for quarters and pennies. She's not going to break Curt's twenty, not until she has to. She'll find a job.

Soon Peanut's curls are down on the table, one tendril purple-edged from a small puddle of juice by her left cheek. When she was just born, Peanut's hair was strange, soft and dark. Curt was blond, and Darlene more red than anything. Curt teased Darlene, where'd she come from, peanut papoose? Now Peanut's a curly girl, red-blond, a combination of them both, for certain. She is out cold. It's been a long morning, and Peanut has been singing most of it like a little robin, ecstatic to be out on the road with her mom.

"What a cutey," says a cool voice. Blondie is back with a dish rag and is trailed by a Suit Guy, wanting to mop off mother and daughter from the now crowded cafe tables. Time to hit the bricks.

"Let her sleep. She won't hurt anything for another half hour." The man, younger than Curt, but dressed in a charcoal suit and red tie like a news anchor, sits down. Blondie shrugs and moves her rag to the next table.

Darlene doesn't meet his eyes. She shoves back the wire chair, ignores the pickup line, and straightens her skirt.

"It's okay, I'm the manager," he says. "What's her name?"

If he'd asked for Darlene's name, Darlene would have gone right on out. But she sees his name tag, James Kincaid, manager, and Bonnie's Viands below it. She sits back down, fortunately, because she's slipped out of one shoe and her feet are swollen.

"Patricia," she tells him softly; Peanut stirs and frowns in her sleep. James slips a cloth napkin over the purple puddle. "I'm Darlene. We call her Peanut, I mean my husband and I do. Most other people do, too."

So he knows she isn't out on the town without someone hovering in the background. Then she is embarrassed; would he think she was pretending she needed protection?

"That'll stain, you know," she says. James shrugs. "I mean, my husband is back at home but we're in town looking for work. I mean I'm looking, Peanut's going to stay with her grandfolks," she lies glibly, "only she can't today. We're just looking around today."

The young man blinks a few time, absorbing these interesting facts and non-facts, as Darlene wonders what kind of introduction that was anyway.

She has been all over the mall this morning, once she found Kids Time Out for Peanut. The two of them had skulked around, scoping out the shoppers and kids traipsing, then the little girl spied the toys through the large plate glass front and Peanut was sold.

"Me!" she pointed at a brightly painted corner with yellow Tonka earth movers and huge pillows and a small toddler sucking his thumb, caressing a corner of the curtain. So Darlene deposited

Peanut, to the tune of ten dollars, and they would waive some of it if she was back by noon and because it was her first time.

The mall building personnel office gave her an application for a janitress job, but they said she had to be bonded, which meant fingerprinted. Darlene made an excuse that she had to plug a meter and hurried off. She doesn't want Curt to find her right away. She is suspicious of leaving her fingerprints, because she knows that the state troopers have computers. She has a notion that tracing fingerprints is a matter of hours these days. Would the police come out to her house to look for traces of her? Of course, her traces will be all over the place. She imagines Curt, white-faced, as the detectives peer into the dishes cupboard, pick up a glass from the strainer, and hold it to the window. Will it be the one she grabbed last night, itching to throw it at Curt? She didn't of course.

After the building personnel office, she tried the specialty shops. They said to try next month when school is out. But that's why, partly why, she thought she should come now, to get ahead of the high school and college summer applicants. That, and the impossibility of spending one more day with Curt.

Most of this tale of woe, with the exception of any reference to Curt, she relates to James the Manager, with an occasional glance at Blondie, who appears sympathetic too. One of the specialty shop people, she tells them, suggested that she try the restaurants.

"You don't want to work at them," he says. "Hustling heavy trays, dodging crabby customers, low pay."

She wonders why he is bad-mouthing his own business. She studies Blondie, ringing up a coffee and roll, and looks questioningly at James. He must be bright, she thinks; he looks like a college kid, short haircut and round glasses perched on a stub nose, but now she sees creases around his eyes. Maybe he's not younger than Curt.

"Oh this place is much better," he winks over at Blondie, who turns her back and arranges glass cups in a rack. "Quiet and small, but all the tables are out on the walkway, so you have room to move. All we sell are salads, desserts, drinks. You polish the glass, ring up the orders, smile at the customers, that's all you have to do." He raises his eyebrows and spreads his hands, presenting this platter of attractions in employment, apparently for Darlene's approval.

"Are you offering me a job?" It couldn't be so easy, but maybe she's lucked out.

"Hold on a minute. Have to see if you're qualified, I've got bosses too, you know. Let's see your pretty smile."

Darlene clicks down her coffee cup decisively and once again begins to pile herself together. Just a lech, she thinks. At the shock to the table, Peanut startles and begins to whimper, her eyes still closed, but she subsides when she feels Darlene's hand on her head. Peanut's hair calms Darlene, too. She looks up at James, challenging.

"You're pretty quick on the trigger, Darlene," he says. Curt used those same words during the fight last night; it stops her for a minute. James's eyes are friendly behind the grandpa glasses. "You know, you have to be cooler to make it in the business world. Give and take, you know?"

He has a point. She isn't cool, not even like Blondie, who apparently can shrug off the passes, if that's what they are, just the daily adversities. Ignore them, as she had ignored, following her mother's advice, her older brothers. Her two brothers, if they noticed her at all when she was little, would generally try to get her goat. They knew how to do it: Pull her braids, call her knock-knees (she shouldn't wear short skirts), throw open the bathroom door when she was on the pot and yell, fire! or, did you feel a draft?

So she is offered and takes the job on probation, five an hour, five-fifty if she stays three months. Only she has to start today and put Peanut back in Kids Time, because Blondie, whose name is really Jean, needs a substitute for a few hours. Blondie-Jean has another job as an answering service for doctors, and her doctors are collecting money for some poor kids in another country.

"I'm the answering service weekends, so this is just extra," Jean explains in the employee's lounge, where they have retired after parking Peanut, to fit Darlene for a uniform. "I just have to pick up some checks, so I'll be back. They're Middle East kids," she says, looking closely at Darlene, "but the donations are legal."

"Good deal," Darlene mumbles, hoping she is not being hit up. She's seen pictures on television of such children, one, in fact, about Peanut's age, who was lying in a crib. She couldn't tell whether the child was a boy or a girl; that one was gray-faced, with dark curly hair and dark eyes open and unblinking. No child should look that sick. The announcer explained that the water was bad.

It isn't that she wouldn't like to donate. God knows, even after moving to the country, she sees poor kids. They come in the mail, pictures of skinny kids with big eyes, or she sees them on television or even on the reservation and in Star Prairie itself. But she and Curt have nothing to spare.

Fortunately, Jean doesn't mention a donation. Most of Darlene's salary today will go to Kids Time, so she will have to find some other kind of care for Peanut later. She is unprepared for the queasiness this thought brings; she has not yet had any morning sickness. Until this last week, the baby came second, probably third, in her thoughts. Peanut and Curt have filled her whole sight and then some.

Darlene has to wear a dumb short Western outfit and do up her hair in a pony tail, like a kid. Jean tells her, as she helps pull Darlene's somewhat thin straight hair through a leather barrette, that the style is supposed to be sexy, supposed to remind you of a rear end.

"A horse's ass is sexy?" Darlene's voice is filled with wonder and disbelief. Jean laughs at her, though not in an unkind way, and steps back to admire. A leather vest over a black sweater flips out prettily over Darlene's breasts, and she has chosen a miniskirt because the optional shorts don't want to close over her slight baby-swell. She perches her fanny pack on her hipbone, so it can look like a holster; she is too careful to let it out of her sight. Even in the brushed steel mirror of the employee's rest room she looks fantastic, Darlene and Jean agree. "Just don't bend over," Jean advises, "somebody drops a fork, squat down."

The work is easy at first. Jean shows her the computer cash register keys in five minutes before she leaves, and James is not around all the time. Once or twice he comes to check on her and asks her to polish the coffee urn or straighten the cases whenever the customers dwindle. There's a bit of bending and stretching associated with the cleaning, but whenever she looks over at James he is not actually watching her at that minute. She can't catch him.

She polishes vigorously, because she can make the new glass and metal cases shine in a way she can't at home, what with the old kitchen and the dirt Peanut and Curt bring in. As the hours poke on, she notices that she is positively light-headed; a headache waxes and wanes, depending on whether she thinks of Curt.

Once, she asks James if he'll take over while she runs down to Peanut with the Pooh book, forgotten on the table in their rush at noon. She's in time to avert disaster. This day that began in disaster may yet turn out well.

* * *

"Pee den Pooh," Peanut kept insisting that morning, swinging her feet up and down to clack on her car seat in time with her words. "Pee den Pooh!"

"In a minute, honey," Darlene temporized; they were ten miles escaped from home but five from the nearest gas station, which was none the cleanest but would have to do.

"Pooh?" Peanut reached for the picture book on the pile next to Darlene. Darlene almost handed it to her but she was afraid of the results.

"Pee *then* Pooh," Darlene said emphatically, without taking her eyes off the road to see the corners of Peanut's mouth turn down in the way that devastated her admirers like her daddy. By this time in her training, Peanut could wait a few minutes. It wasn't a real emergency, not like two nights ago when the disaster began.

Two nights ago, Jerry Young Wolf, Curt's supposed enemy, called her in the middle of the night to pick up Curt from Star Lake. Something happened to the Toyota. Curt was all right, Wolf said, but his voice was funny when he said it, so she should have known Curt was drunk.

And why Wolf had waited with Curt, she'd never understand. It wasn't just for a lift to the reservation. The spearfishing Indians and their supporters had gone home and, except for Curt, the local white group protesting the early catch had given up. The landing was deserted except for the pair of them, Curt sitting at a picnic table, holding his head in his hands, and Wolf standing behind him, his bulky form wrapped in a sensible Hudson Bay blanket. Early May at midnight in the woods was not like May in town. A lone squad car sat next to Curt's Toyota, the squad's interior lights casting a faint yellow onto the sparse growth and trampled mud of the boat access. The squad waited for Wolf's all-right wave, then bumped onto the highway and drove off.

Darlene stayed put in the pickup. She had to unbuckle Peanut from her carseat and free her with one arm; with the other, she dumped the child's seat in the narrow space behind the front seat. Wolf steadied Curt onto the seat next to Darlene, then climbed in, reaching over Curt to take Peanut in his arms. "The Center," he told her, "Someone will take me from there."

In the pickup that night, Peanut started saying the words, Pee den Pooh, sleepily but with a whiny edge that grew in volume. Wolf thought it a strange maybe Indianlike word, Peedenpoo. Darlene explained, whispering across Curt's stuporous body, though why she bothered to whisper, the jerk! she didn't know. Anyway she told Wolf about how Peanut loved Winnie the Pooh and she, Darlene, invented the game. Peanut would pee then Darlene would read Pooh to her.

Wolf said it was a good way. Peanut kept on whimpering, because the book was back at home. She had dutifully piddled before Darlene bundled her out to the pickup, and now there was no Pooh! So Wolf wrapped his stocky arms around her squirming and told her a story about a real bear. The real bear whose name was Bear and not Winnie, lived in the woods near Wolf's house at White Earth. Wolf wasn't from Star Prairie but was of the same nation as the St. Croix band doing the fishing. He came down each year to witness and pray for the endeavor.

Bear, Wolf said, came to live near Wolf's house one summer and began to lick the early July blueberries off the bushes at the edge of the wood, curling his nimble tongue around the fat juicy ones.

Every morning Bear licked them, before Wolf could come out with his pail to pick them. Wolf saw Bear's tracks in the morning dew, so he knew who had done it. Wolf decided he would pick all the early ones he could find, even the small pale blue hard ones; but some were sour and didn't ripen in the house and Wolf had a tummyache. Bear ate the later ones and felt fine. So they had a talk.

Darlene stole a look at Peanut's half-lidded eyes, wondering how much she understood. "Blue juice," Peanut mumbled. Wolf and Bear, said Wolf, agreed to share. Wolf would pick berries in the daytime, but he would leave some good ones for Bear's visits. "And they lived happily together?" Darlene wanted to add, but Wolf shushed her. Peanut's eyes were closed.

Peanut slept until they dropped Wolf at the Reservation Center, but the cold air of his leaving woke her. He eased her head onto her father's legs and fastened the seat belt around her waist, before he closed the pickup door, as softly as he could. Peanut fussed on and off the rest of the miles home, while Darlene drove slowly, peering past her headlights for the twin gleam of animal eyes. Naturally, Curt never knew a thing.

Darlene waited until the next day, yesterday, to have it out with Curt. That Star Lake night he was in no condition; she herself pushed him down on the couch, where he'd sat stunned and sick, and pulled a comforter over him. Sometime during the night he'd undressed to his jockey shorts, leaving a smelly pile of jeans and shirts on the floor. In the morning she swept by, scooping the pile into a bundle of dark clothes, on her way to the basement. Makeup stained his collar, and everything smelled of booze and fish. Fish?

He wasn't supposed to be fishing. He'd gone to protest the Indians' spring spearfishing, he said, with the guys; he said it was for Peanut, for their future in Star Prairie. Now there is no future, she has left for good.

The fight, explanation he tried to call it, went on all day, between silences, between when she slammed outside to mow the front lawn herself because he said he had a headache and she said serve him right. She didn't feel that great herself, and had her regular clinic appointment to go to that afternoon, and then he wouldn't listen to what the doctor had said.

Later, Curt told her, yes, it was this girl Nancy's makeup and he and Nancy shared a tuna sandwich, that was the smell, but it wasn't like that, he said. Like what? she wanted to know. What was it like? He said they just talked. Nancy was a spearfishing supporter but not an Indian. She came up from the Cities to be a witness. They dialogued, because they had different opinions.

Oh yeah *di*alogue, that's what you call Passion Pink lipstick all over your shirt front, Darlene said. He said he was helping Nancy out, it was asscold on the landing; Darlene said something rude about *his* ass and he slammed out the back door.

It wasn't the worst fight they'd ever had but thinking about it while she drove Peanut wasn't good. She remembers she tried to put Curt away from her thoughts then, but it was difficult. He was about to tell her what to do, driving down the road; she was about to ask him. She tried to pull the blinds on Curt in her mind, but he kept peeking through, mocking and angry. What the hell do you think you're doing, Darlene? She remembers she kept having to ease her foot on the accelerator. He'd be sorry if they were in an accident, wouldn't he? getting the call, turning pale: Where? how could it be?

Wolf had whispered to her in the pickup, while Peanut and Curt slept, that Curt wasn't in danger at Star Lake. The car was just stuck, only it was a little close to the edge of the overlook. Darlene wondered. Curt said, during the fight, that the Indians didn't have to ding up the Toyota getting them out. Darlene countered that the Indians didn't have to pull them out at all.

"What, they're going to push us over the edge?" Curt yelled. "Jesus, they're human!"

She shot him a victory gesture, thumb and forefinger in a circle, got that right, dumb shit. She guessed that was snotty. Of course she was glad he wasn't hurt.

The service station appeared in the nick of time, almost too late to judge by Peanut's dancing steps to the door. It was locked, naturally. She hoisted Peanut on a hip, a danger to her good skirt, and swung around the corner to collect the key.

"Gas today?" the sour-faced young guy behind the glass cage asked. The station was a modern SuperAmerica, robber-proofed, walling in its employees, so she didn't blame him for his fishy look and bad mood. Could she work in a place like that, like a cell? She curled her hand under the scooped-out pass-through for the key. Peanut thought that was very interesting, and stopped her hip-bouncing to regard the man somberly. Then the guy mashed his face right up to the glass, pursing and blowing his lips like a real fish, sending everyone into giggles. Almost everybody had a good side, Darlene thought, especially around little kids.

Then the mood was spoiled when they pulled out of the station. Peanut spotted a slumped shape on the side of the road, one paw stretched out of the mass of fur, its naked black pads turned skyward, as if asking something.

" 'Zat?" she asked, pointing.

"Poor raccoon."

"'Coon sleepy," Peanut determined, satisfied. Darlene didn't correct her: Darlene saw the matted hair and red near the road edge and thought it had happened recently, within the last hour. She knew, however, that she didn't hit the animal because she'd been with Curt when that happened and there is always a small thump, a heavy live feel you can't miss, not like hitting a rock.

Two nights ago, even though she'd been concentrating on driving, she caught sight of several odd gestures Jerry Young Wolf made to the passenger side window. Finally she got up the nerve to ask him what he was doing.

"It's something I do for the death," he told her, "for the spirit."

"Dead animals?' she asked, wanting to believe.

"Relatives," he half-smiled, to ease the seriousness of her question.

That raccoon this morning was not even a tender adolescent coon specimen, inexperienced or brashly testing its powers against a strip of cement. He — or she? — was in full glossy pride, probably loping along in the early morning looking for food for itself or its young. Like herself, actually. She pondered the smash of civilization against dumb animals, individually and collectively. Not a fair fight, to the Death, for mating or territory like on Wild Kingdom, but an invisible, inexorable machine pounding a life into oblivion. Blotted out, red blot on the side of the road. As she said to Wolf, it really wasn't fair. What had he said? "Fair is a word for children."

As she drove slowly by the raccoon this morning, she tried to imitate Wolf's graceful motion; was it like the sign of the cross? An old woman fishing in a mailbox next to the road, maybe fifty feet away from the dead animal, gave her a puzzled wave. Darlene sputtered with laughter, her heart climbing back up, and drove on.

* * *

Toward six o'clock, when she'll have to pick up Peanut, she arranges the remaining chocolate concoctions on the top shelf, admiring their extravagant shapes. Peanut would go ape over them, but at two-fifty a crack, there's no way Darlene can afford them. One sweet looks like a tiny hamburger, a chocolate wafer with red and yellow icing spilling between two vanilla buns. Another more elongated bun wraps a pink marshmallow tube similarly decorated with red and yellow squiggles lacing specks of green candied fruit: hot dog with mustard, catsup, piccalilli. And one larger one represents a gorgeously colored gold- and red-scaled shiny fish, with glaucous but sugary eyes.

Curt wouldn't listen to her about the fish. He thought she was making it up just for purposes of the fight. But she wasn't. "Chrissake, Darlene, fish has got to be good for you, all that protein." They ate fish all the time, Curt reminded her, it was their staple food and it cut down on the grocery bill. Their landlady's freezer was full of walleye.

"They're poisoned with mercury, from the water, the doctor said," Darlene insisted. "They don't recommend, especially children, pregnant mothers . . . " She was trying to be cool and clear; there was no reason for the tears sliding down her face.

"Recommend shit. It's natural food, the Indians eat it all the time, don't they? What harm can it do?"

She tried to remember the doctor's exact words. "Neuro something damage. Muscle trembles, fetal abnormalities." That was what got her, that was why she had to make Curt see.

But then Curt told her she had to be sensible and not listen to every quack theory. But he looked so desperate, she remembers, as if the fish were more than fish to him.

The shimmering white eye stares at her from the glass case. Why is she sitting on the floor? James is patting her wrist and Jean, back for her next shift, is holding a damp cloth to Darlene's forehead.

"When are we going to eat? What's going on?" Darlene doesn't know what she is doing on the floor, so the questions are the first ones that come into her mind. The others lift and practically carry her to a table, although she tries to tell them she can walk, she is just a little dizzy.

"I don't know," Jean is the one who answers. "We hear this slithery noise and next thing we see your head sliding down in back of the case and you disappear."

James says, "Maybe something spilled and you slipped. Why don't you go check if the floor's wet, Jean?" He keeps patting Darlene's wrist, awkwardly. Jean gives him a look and says, "She fainted, that's all. You eat anything today, honey?"

"Fish," she murmurs, shaking her head, "I was thinking about fish. No, Peanut ate, though, at Kids Time. That was good." Darlene has never fainted in her life. "Maybe I forgot my iron pill, I'm supposed to . . . " She rummaged in the fanny pack for her prescription bottle, which bears the name of the clinic, Prenatal Care, bold enough for Jean to spy.

"You're pregnant," Jean accuses her.

"Not much," Darlene grins, "just a little minnow." So they all laugh and calm the situation. James admires her spirit. He declares she can have extra hours tomorrow if she goes home and gets some rest, but Darlene knows she won't be back tomorrow. Curt is worried about her.

She realizes it, just now. Curt may be a poor fish sometimes, but he's her relative too. She realizes Curt thinks he has to take care of her. Maybe he really does believe her about the fish, only he's too worried to say it. She can make him believe it, anyhow, because she knows what she's talking about. She can do almost anything if she puts her spirit into it — didn't she decide to leave and get a job, and didn't she do it? No matter she's changing her mind, that's part of it. She can change Curt's mind, too, dialogue with him. Maybe Curt can be as good at planting a garden as he is at planting babies. She'll suggest it to him.

Of the three crisp tens James gives her in an envelope, Darlene saves one for Kids Time and one for a steak dinner for herself and Peanut, before they drive back. Charity begins at home.

The third one she presses into Jean's hand for the bad-water babies in the Middle East. "You can't," Jean stammers, but stops when she encounters Darlene's glare. "It's very generous, you'll get a note for taxes. . . . Where should we send it?"

At first, Darlene waves her off, then writes down their address in Star Prairie on an official donation form. She can't wait to see Curt's face when the thank-you comes.

In the General Population, in Ordinary Time

The building is a disappointment. Squat and spread-eagled over a small ragged plot, the Women's Section is a poor cousin to the fortress next door. The Men's Section, set like a monument on its vast treeless grounds, looms dark and sooty as any urban jail, and wears the bleak spyglass windows of guard towers. The Men's can house four hundred: tiers of cages face a common multi-storied hall. The Women's holds one-tenth that many, although Jen knows it is overcrowded these days, short-term women sleeping in the day room on weekends.

Two wings with opaque windows flank a central square structure, all facing the road; behind these, a longer protuberance juts into the vacant fields. Across the fields, a row of suburban bungalows shield their backs with hedges and moderately expensive landscaping. The Women's could be some sort of small machine factory, or a processing plant. Yes, the latter is what it is: I will be processed, Jen thinks; I will follow the procedures.

Jen's been in jail before, but served only the standard sentence for trespassers, two days on a short-term lock-up, in the company of other activists. Now she'll be with others, the regular prisoners, will eat and drink and talk with them. She is not frightened; what's to fear from boredom, and from doing as you are told in a locked building?

She is, however, depressed.

Jail wasn't part of her plans for this week — or month. Bastard. He didn't have to do it. Sitting up there like lord almighty, yes, you did get the hanging judge, he says. She'd tried to be respectful, even used the word, must respectfully refuse to pay the fine. She'd dressed up for court, squeezed into a dark dress from her secretarial days, nylons, and the heels she wouldn't even wear to church. She'd surrendered the comfort of warm picket-line slacks and sweaters, to look respectable and respectful. In conscience, your honor, I can't pay a fine. Can't, or won't? he asks. The court takes indigence into account. She tells him she isn't indigent, it's a matter of conscience, but she isn't eloquent enough. She mentions that fines do discriminate, but what he doesn't like is that she says she won't buy her way out. Thirty days, he says, contempt of court. But I'm not being contemptuous, she argues. The judge stops listening, motions to the bailiff. She has a minute to talk to Bob; but even her usually supportive husband has a comment about her timing, before he kisses her good-bye.

She wants to take in the outside air — the day crowding down in swollen clouds, dark grays, with a tang of snow. It's been a dry season. Leaves are powder under her feet and the dust from them hazes the sky over Parker's Lake, just across the road. It's been hours since she was outside, free, and an hour of that morning time was spent on the bus downtown, with its tired air. She couldn't sit next to Bob, and the man next to her was so big half of Jen's right hip, no slouch itself, was perched on nothing. She could scarcely read for all the jouncing around. They probably won't give her the book, inside, because it has a hard cover and could harbor something dangerous — drugs, a stick of gum.

Now there is moisture in the wind and on the sides of the grimy van — a smear of soot lines her forearm as she hitches herself down. A few fat flakes of snow fall like raindrops and disappear into the grass.

"Come on." The driver carefully piles her coat, boots, and a grocery bag containing her purse, book, and intake papers into Jen's outstretched arms. Then he unlocks her handcuffs; nothing spills. He puts a hand under one elbow: uncuffed, her arm needs custody, she thinks. She might make a break for it, dash to the lake and spin pebbles onto the singing film of ice and listen to the mystery of it until evening.

In the shower room, she steps out of her clothes and away from her body. Ms. Mackenzie, as the guard's name tag reads, watches her and hands her another grocery bag for her clothing.

"Fold them. They'll have to stay in the bag until they're checked overnight."

Jen focuses on the clock above Mackenzie's head, but listens to the instructions. Her body is obedient, unembarrassed, Jen notes with approval. I'm invisible, she thinks, no, opaque. I'm here but my body tells her nothing; the guard can't see inside me. Jen can still do three deep knee bends without trembling. Lifting her hair so that Mackenzie can peer behind her ears, though, is more intimate. Abruptly Jen is inside her nakedness, and sees the pale hairs on her arms stand with the goosebumps.

At dinnertime, the lights flicker. The televisions, three of them in a large and small day room, and in the dormitory hall, have been tuned to warnings all afternoon.

White letters slide under Alex Keaton's dimples and all through "Jeopardy." A fenced exercise yard is visible from the dining area windows, and it begins to fill with snow, wet and lumpy at first, but soon turning mean and dry, spinning with a shrill wind. The guards are jumpy, those going off work at six wanting to get on the road.

After she has been hurried through the line, Jen has to start a new table, so she doesn't have anyone to practice her icebreaker on. She's going to say, Nice night to be Inside. But by the time other women join her, she's decided against it.

At 5:30 the lights flicker twice. The women exclaim and laugh: something is really happening. The conversation swells until a hasty conference of guards decides it's an emergency, they're going to be short-handed tonight.

"All right, ladies. Room time. Finish up, clear your plates. Last table, stand, take your dishes."

Guards Parris and Bordman, two male guards assigned under the new Equal Opportunity rules, come and stand by the scraping table as the women stack their plates. "Go immediately to your wing," they say, unnecessarily, Jen thinks. This is unfair; room time shouldn't be for hours yet. She hears the women grumbling, but there's no time for discussion.

She's just begun to eat, so she's swallowing fast. A stout woman at the next table is still hunched over her coffee. She appears to hear nothing. She has just come in tonight, and has the stunned, sullen inattention of a newcomer, except that she draws away more

noticeably from contact. One hand is taped, and one brown cheek
is purplish black from bruising.

"Jones," Parris addresses her. She doesn't look up.

"Jones! Up, now!" The woman starts and gives him a sidelong
glance. "I ain't finished my coffee." She's nervous but belligerent;
she lowers her head to blow on the cup, admittedly still steaming.
Jen thinks maybe this is the way to be, stand your ground.

Parris jerks his head at Bordman, who comes to second him.

"Come on, Betsy. You don't want more trouble."

Jen's the last in line at the trash bucket, scraping her plate, so
she sees what happens next. Betsy panics and wraps her plump
legs around her chair, so it comes along when the men attempt
to hoist her. The chair screeches, then clatters to the floor as they
scoot her along.

Bordman is half laughing; he's muscular and the woman isn't
really offering much resistance, just yelling, "no, no, you got no
right!" It's only twenty feet down the hall to the first cell, which
is a separation cell.

That night, the banging begins. Bordman and then Parris move
to Betsy's door to yell, or to try to talk reasonably to her, by turns.
She'd better shape up or she's in separation through Thanksgiving.
Sounds of objects hitting the floor, and Bordman's laugh, carry
down to Jen's cell. She flattens her face against the ten-inch open-
ing in the steel door, but she can't put her head through, and the
angle's wrong. She's three cells down, on the same side. A few
minutes later, she can just see a barricade the guards put up to
shield the patrols from flying objects. Jen can't imagine what could
be left in the cell to throw. Her own cell has no movable furniture
except the desk chair and bedding; bed, desk, and sink are bolted
to the floor or wall, as is the steel mirror, which rather pleasantly
masks her wrinkles and flaws. For a while she imagines Betsy
dismantling her cell tile by tile to toss at the hallway.

Then Betsy begins knocking. She starts off with a string of in-
sults, names for the guards, focusing on their weight problems:
blubberbutt, blimpo, or other physical characteristics, which Jen
thinks could do wonders for her own vocabulary. A few people
on the wing shout to cool it, mama, you in bad trouble, but Betsy's
sounds come only wilder and sadder. Through the gradual quieting
of other noises on the cellblock, Betsy bangs on the wall or the

door. She doesn't stop. She continues a regular, sometimes muffled, sometimes hollow pounding that goes on and on, a patient, hopeless, defiant sound that quiets her listeners.

Down the hall, someone calls to the guard but Jen thinks they've left the area. Nobody can be hurt now; the prisoners are all safe in their cells.

Jen's throat aches with wanting to yell something; she finally does, "Please stop!" but her voice is thin and ineffectual. She decides silence and waiting are best. Still it doesn't stop.

Jen couldn't let her babies cry it out. She remembers deciding to time their nighttime fussing after she'd put them down, but she never had done that. The watch hands wouldn't move. Picking up the baby after what must have been only minutes, she'd rock him again. And again. When she'd calmed herself, rocking, the baby slept. Now she doesn't have a watch, anyway. What's the point of taking away our watches? she wonders. We're going to hang ourselves on our watchbands? Swallow them? Tiny ticking machines in our stomachs, marking the moments, timing, doing time. . . .

Five minutes can seem forever, she knows. Probably Jones hadn't been banging that long, but now Jen's head throbs. The trouble is, she can't do anything about this situation. She's powerless. Maybe she can pray for Jones, for Betsy. Concentrating her thought, Jen pictures Betsy in her cell, the extra large pink jogging suit from the clothing room pushed back on her thick arms, her face, sweaty and heavy with fatigue, her wide-fingered black hand fisting a shoe — it must be a shoe — knocking it against the door. Jen tries to imagine the creator of Betsy calming her, stopping her impossible protest and bringing peace and quiet to the rest of them.

But the noise doesn't stop. Jen is dismayed to feel her resentment turn to something uglier; she thinks specifically of breaking Betsy's wrist. God isn't anywhere, and Jen's heart hammers faster than Betsy's noise. Breathe, she tells herself, breathe; she'll be okay, you'll be okay.

The next morning she approaches Mackenzie, sitting by herself at the end of the wing hall. All the cell doors are open, including the separation room, which is empty. In fact, Betsy had been at breakfast queening over a crowded table of African-American dormitory women who talk low and fast, giggling like conspirators.

Dormitory is a misnomer; the women do not sleep in one room, but have individual cells containing one cot, one student desk, one chair, and one hook. The dormitory wing is identical to Jen's, except that the cells do not contain their own toilets or washbowls, which are in a common lavatory on one end of the wing. Besides not having to sleep three feet from a toilet, the advantage of the dormitory is that the women are not locked in their cells but only into the wing, during the night.

Mackenzie tells her that Betsy is a long-termer, not a newcomer as Jen thought. She's been in long enough to have had a day pass for a family emergency, except that she took three weeks. They had to bring her back.

"Is that how she got the bruises?" Jen believes she's overstepping her bounds, but the question presses at her. She wants to redeem her uncharitable reactions of last night, if only for herself. She doesn't remember when the knocking became the rhythm of her own heartbeat, but she fell easily into sleep, and slept well.

Mackenzie is curt. "No. Family, I think. The health officer saw her. She's all right."

Betsy is more than all right, she's back to work in the laundry room. They can hear her, as a nervous line of weekenders deposit bedding inside the laundry room door, one by one, and bustle back to their stripped cells to clean them.

"In the *whites,* bitch! You separate them now." Jen hears a querulous defensive answer and scornful, "Sheeit!" from Betsy. Mackenzie looks toward the laundry door but doesn't move.

"You check your job yet?"

Jen had forgotten. "Oh, right." It was part of the intake instructions; she was supposed to check the job chart posted outside the kitchen door, right after breakfast.

Mackenzie gives her a brief smile. "First day." She consults a clip board on her lap. "Okay. Soon as you're done, go back to your cell and strip your bed. We're moving you into the dormitory."

Jen is alarmed, but wants to keep the mood light. "Okay. Is this a promotion?"

Mackenzie narrows her eyes. "Not exactly. We like to keep the one wing for short termers, DWIs, weekenders. You're technically with general population."

Technically. Encouraged, Jen thinks she can try to be political. "You know why I'm here?"

But Mackenzie closes down. "Everybody knows. But listen to me. Nobody thinks they should be here, you understand? My job is to take care of your needs. I don't ask anybody why they're in, it don't matter. And I don't care. I do a better job that way. And you, you will too, understand?"

Jen nods, and moves away. All this and lectures, too. Does that mean she should keep her mouth shut? Everybody knows, nobody cares? They must think she can handle herself in the dormitory, but what does that mean?

The chart says Jen is supposed to mop the day room. The mop buckets are already taken, or so Betsy tells her when she looks into the laundry room. So Jen begins to straighten *True Confessions* and *Plain Truth* magazines in the day room, where she will have a vantage point on the laundry room door. When she reaches the lower shelves, she pulls a chair over to them and sits down, trying not to look too comfortable. But Mr. Ward, the cook, pokes his head in from the kitchen and beckons to her. "What are you supposed to be doing?"

She stands up. Respectful, always respectful. "Mopping. Buckets are gone."

He turns away. "Wait for one."

She sighs and turns back to the magazines. "Not here!" he yelps.

Ms. Mackenzie comes in from the hall as Jen tries to leave the day room. "So what's going on now?"

Mr. Ward lights a cigarette.

"I'm waiting," Jen says, patiently, glancing at the cook; he's waiting, we're all waiting, she thinks, for my next words. "For a bucket."

She thinks she says it patiently; but Mackenzie steps in very close. "There are three buckets in the laundry room. You take one, you mop this room and the kitchen, you return the bucket, clean it out, and you do not get written up again today."

There are indeed three full buckets in the laundry room, returned in the last thirty seconds like magic. Betsy's broad back is turned to the door, and she's humming as she gathers warm towels and bedspreads into her arms from the dryer. "Any special one I should take?"

Betsy looks around. "Not my business." Then as Jen is hauling
the full pail and wringer into the hall, she adds, "Sugarbabe you
supposed to get *clean* water if you do the kitchen!"

Jen flushes; my god, the ptomaine kid. That water definitely had
seen clearer days. Betsy points her to the floor drain and to the
shelf where the detergent and vinegar are kept. She also points
out that girl scout isn't in her job description.

* * *

Jen awakes. When had she fallen asleep? It must have been before
the television in the dormitory hall had gone off at lights-out,
because the last sounds she remembers are gunshots from some
police story, the third in a row, Jesus, didn't they get enough of
that in their real lives? But we have to miss the ten o'clock news,
after lights-out, so at least we miss that violence, she thinks. Jen
couldn't have heard about the latest demonstrations, either. Well,
maybe it was for the best. Night after night, she had been so tired.
The slogans still echo in her head, louder here against the
background noise, the constant television. No more killing, no
more war, U.S. out of El Salvador.

She twists away from the sudden glare. The flashlight circle
sweeps down her body and disappears. A few seconds later, she
hears a groan and curse from next door. Guard rounds. Is it near
morning? No light from the window. More people die just before
dawn than at any other time. That's probably a myth, but her body
is indeed stiffening, cramping. It's so cold. She sits up, far enough
to reach her day clothes on the hook above the bed and pulls them
down over the covers. The extra weight helps a little; the warmth
spreads and soothes her. She won't think of Bob, not yet. After
all, she was used to turning down the thermostat at night, used
to cold sheets they kicked at, laughing, daring each other to be
first inside. The first could be charitable and warm the other's side
before sliding over. How often had she been the charitable one?

Jen wonders how many women in here put themselves to sleep
warming their hands between their thighs, timing it between guard
rounds, how often? Most, she supposes, but she doesn't want to,
not now, it's too sad. She won't cry.

The next night is worse. The cells are no longer cold, though; men have been on the wing tinkering with the heat system, and the furnace blasts through with ancient dust and metallic-smelling air. Because of the repair work, the prisoners have had no room time during the day, and have been packed into the day room and told to watch television quietly. Jen's eyes itch from all the television and from the cigarettes, but she's just not tired. She hasn't had a job all day except to clean ashtrays, which took maybe ten minutes. She tried to talk to Patrice, a bright forger with a coke habit, about Jen's work publicizing Contragate, and the evidence about U.S. guns traded for Contra drugs. Patrice's eyes widened, but she countered with a fantastic rumor about Administration marijuana ranches. Jen worried, "Well, maybe that's a little exaggeration, but . . . "

"Just say no, ha!" Patrice shook her head and wandered off.

Now too warm, the cell smells of stale smoke and Lysol. She decides to open the window, a lower casement that pulls inward and opens directly on a steel mesh screen and the November air. As she kicks back the latch, a rustle outside and a sudden shadow make her jump. Someone is standing by the window! The whir of a dozen pair of large wings reassure her: Canada geese rise in the moonlight and settle twenty feet away, silent but standing in profile to her. Their two lookouts pace between the window and the flock, wary. As she crouches to see them better, cold fresh air washes her shoulders. The lake must still be open, or maybe the geese will winter here; she hopes so, they'll be something to look at. In a few seconds they are still again, nestled near some low shrubs, though the lookouts are open-eyed and standing erect.

The wall beside her brightens. "Hey! Close that window! Those windows stay closed at night!"

Jen knows that is not a rational rule, and if she had the energy, she might be assertive about it. But the light plays on her nightgown until she closes the window, so she does it quickly and slips back into bed.

The cell is already becoming stuffy again. She throws off the blanket. Hot rooms at night give her nightmares, and she feels the uneasiness of a bad night coming on. If only her thoughts would line up obediently to be sorted and processed, she would sleep better. She has a civilly disobedient brain.

If only she hadn't argued with her friend Anne, so many months ago, Anne might come to see her. Who would come, on visiting days? Most people would think a month wasn't so long; she could take it. You had to be ready to take consequences, just a little piece of your life, that's all. For your friends. Not that she was doing this work for Anne, or for some religious principle. It was closer than that. Of course it was selfish, sure, it was her own children who made her look at weapons and weaponmakers with the sick dread she held for rapists or molesters. And then she looked long and hard at pictures of the Salvadoran and Nicaraguan children, this decade's victims, those beautiful dark eyes, and the blood.

But Anne, how could she? Maybe she didn't want to be a church counselor any more, but applying to Federal Munitions, in Human Resources? Human she said. She said Jen didn't give her credit for thinking out her decision. Of course I did, Jen thinks, I wanted Anne to tell me why, some misbegotten ministry to the affluent? A good company, Anne said. A death factory, Jen said. Are you going to pay my rent? Anne asked. Oh, shit.

Is that what the women in here want to know, too? Jen wonders. Who's going to pay the rent? Is Jen supposed to have the answers?

Limp pale toast for the third morning, white bread, of course. The oranges run out before Jen's turn in line, and she's given canned peach slices, five of them half afloat in the viscous liquid like lean goldfish. She says so to Vivian, a six-foot tall, red-haired, red-elbowed Louisiana girl who generally has empty chairs around her at mealtime. She leans into people, angry or needy, absorbing others' space like a sponge.

Vivian's smile broadens bony cheeks and her eyes gleam; everything on her face is on fire. "Yeah they look like fish! Lookit," she elbows Patrice, in line behind her, "my fish!"

"Watch it!" Vivian's tray hits Patrice's and a glob of syrup spills just into a splash of sunlight on the formica table. Bits of peach pulp shimmer, and Vivian is enthralled. "Hey, tiny fish. Minnows!"

Patrice snorts and turns away, but Jen smiles. Vivian says, "Hey! I'm gonna write a poem about fish. You know we got a typewriter? You know how to type?"

Jen agrees to type the poem about fish for Vivian's boyfriend. It will pass the time.

The dormitory telephone system works by consensus; Jen

approves. She knows the value of self-regulation and flexibility. But it takes her three days to learn she has to interrupt an established order and insert herself into a time slot convenient to her neighbors.

She asks Chris if she can talk next; Chris tells her Betsy is next; she asks Betsy, and Betsy refers her to Vivian. Vivian says Patrice is next but Patrice is on kitchen duty until 7:00, so maybe Jen can be on the phone list if Vivian can get on the phone by 6:30. The first nights Vivian can't. Betsy hooks her sturdy ankles around her chair legs beside the phone and suggests cheerful immovability for nearly twenty-five minutes. Vivian is next, but when Jen comes to check on Vivian's progress a few minutes later, Betsy is again sprawled on the chair in earnest conversation, her head down.

The next night Jen believes she will wait in the hall near the phone and insist on her turn. Guard Bordman sends her back to her cell. Then she hits on the plan of lurking in the washroom across the hall, and she is in luck. When Vivian finishes her call and is on her way to Betsy's cell to fetch her, Jen grabs the receiver and quickly dials. On the third ring, Vivian and Betsy pass, scowling.

"Hi, honey," Jen says to the still ringing phone, and mouths to Betsy, "I'll tell Patrice when I'm done." She is very pleased with herself. But Bob isn't home.

On the fourth day of Jen's incarceration, she and Vivian attend a GED class in parenting, conducted by a social worker from the county. Vivian is not a mother, but the topic is What is abuse? What is discipline? and Vivian carries the scars from her mother's discipline. Besides, the craft today is making place cards for Thanksgiving, with heavy use of glue and glitter, and Vivian's long bony fingers become graceful in picking bits of glitter from the table and her pants legs.

"I'm gonna put a border around this one, but I'll leave a hole for someone's name."

"Who, Viv?" the social worker asks. None of them will be home for Thanksgiving, but they can send the cards home.

Vivian shrugs.

Jen will send hers to Bob. She'd finally reached him; he's decided to drive down to visit their son at school for the long weekend. But he says, hang in there. She wonders what the alternative is.

None of the women think hitting children is the best discipline, although they admit to having done it under duress.

"What about adults?" Betsy enters the room, late, with piles of clothes for the women there. She wants to describe her recent fight with her husband.

"He thinks he can yell and smack me around, he's got another think coming. I took the extension cord, it was one of those big jobbers, thick, like my thumb, what you call 'em. . . ."

"Utility, uh, heavy duty, those orange ones?" Jen wants to make an accurate contribution to the conversation.

"Maybe, and I reared back and flung it like a lasso; it got him around the neck." She put her own thick hands on her throat and stuck out her tongue to show how it was, him spitting and trying to yell.

"Sure Betsy," Patrice says, "and what's he do to you?"

"What could he do, he's busy trying to breathe and unfasten that cord, his hands was so tied up. . . ."

"Oh you tie him up first," Vivian remarks.

"You shut up girl, you so smart why's your ugly face in here?"

The social worker interrupts, tries to bring them back to children. Since Jen is new, she asks her gently, "What about you, Jen? What do you think?"

Jen frowns. "No, of course I don't think you should punish by hitting." She pauses, remembering. "But you can hurt them other ways too." Then she has no idea how to go on.

"Do you want to tell us?" the worker prods.

She doesn't, really. "Oh, the worst thing maybe is ignoring, not paying attention when they need it, or getting so wrapped up in your own pain. . . ."

She probably won't see these women again in her life. She has their attention; it's something.

"It was a long time ago. Davey, my son, he was still in diapers, but running around. My husband was addicted, and they had just released him, and I couldn't manage." She looks around, and sees heads nod. "I swallowed a bunch of his pills. Davey was playing in the next room, but I couldn't think about him, I wanted someone to take care of *me*."

She stops. It's too complicated to explain about her husband, the death of that marriage and wanting to die. "It was a lot of years ago. Things are better now."

But the social worker asks her to finish. "So what happened?"

"Right after I did it, I stuck my finger down my throat, threw up. All over my in-laws' Aubusson carpet. That was one of the *best* things I ever did."

The five women in the room are staring at her. Betsy hoots. "And now last week you throw blood all over the senator's carpet. You still messy, Jen."

They do know. Jen laughs, "Housekeeping was never one of my strong suits."

After the social worker leaves, they talk about worse things and drugs. Patrice has been careful around the social worker because she wants her children back and the lady is going to write a letter for her to the court. Now she explains to an admiring circle how she passed the last urine test she had, with her little daughter's pee funneled into a balloon. The balloon was tied and tucked into Patrice's skirtband. Her deft fingers weave the story in her lap, how she maneuvered the neck of the balloon into the specimen bottle, slipped the tie onto her finger, and filled the bottle. "The only hard part," she laughs, "is holding back your own pee."

Chris tells about being a cocaine cardiac. "My heart stopped, must of been almost a minute! Ma had called 911, they worked on me when I was out, and they said my heart stopped. I was in County a couple weeks, they say I'll never be able to coach again."

Chris is a tiny Hispanic woman of twenty who volunteers in a girl's program as a basketball coach. She moves as though she's been choreographed, and still has the tight muscled legs of an athlete, but she's restricted from heavy cleaning. Dancing with a broom, she begins to cough, a wheezy kitten sound.

"It's the needle, huh?" Riva asks her. "Crack?" She is afraid of needles herself, because of AIDS. Riva's a cab driver who has been intercepted at the airport and, through an unfortunate error in baggage handling, was discovered to be transporting an illegal substance. She's heavy-set, with the cool light and shadows of the moon in her pretty, pitted face. Her complaint is that she had to double up in the Minneapolis jail with a well-publicized prostitute who does have AIDS. "You know, maybe she has an open sore and there I am sick, with this eczema." Her bare arms are still inflamed. "I yelled all the first day, but you think anybody listens?"

The women nod; they know the disease isn't spread by touch but they leave Riva a lot of space.

That night Jen sleeps soundly, except that an old classroom teacher comes in, shaking his head at her honors paper. 'Hang it up,' he says to her dream self. 'This is new work,' she insists, but her paper is messy, covered with hen tracks and scratching out, dirt. She tries to grab it from him before he can see the drops of blood coursing down the margin.

The next day is Thanksgiving. Special visitors, The Prince of Peace Singers, have come and gone with their Sunday dresses, high hair, and heels clicking back down the corridor, through the gate. The building is quieter, but the dinner has an anticlimactic air. Some of the women have a pass for the day and will be brought back by van from downtown. Jen is late for the meal; for some reason there was no call to dinner. She'd been reading and no one came to call her from her cell.

She turns from the steam table into the dining area; with the reduced population, only the back half of the long room is set up and lit. At the last table, though, she sees an empty chair. She makes for it and puts her tray down. Riva blocks the chair with her arm.

"You can't sit here," she claims, "we're saving a place for Betsy." Jen looks around the table, uncertainly; maybe they'd make room if she pulled up another chair. One or two women look worried but no one moves. Vivian grins, "Hey Betsy'll raise a ruckus, we don't save her place."

It's true. Betsy always sits here, in the last chair, by the window. The dining room is oppressively quiet tonight; even Betsy's table seems subdued. Outside, a tree branch beside the window scratches at the glass, like a dog asking to be let in.

Jen carries her tray to the darkened section and sets it down. She walks to the other end of the room and turns on all the switches. Parris, standing by the door, looks around at the sudden light, but doesn't move or say anything. They could have pulled up another chair, Jen thinks, they just didn't want me there.

It's too much. She doesn't belong here, not even here. There is nothing she can give to these women, to ease the weight of their lives, their desperate needs.

At least there's a box of Kleenex by the light switch and she has her back to the rest of the women. She blows her nose, but the tears keep forming and falling and she has to put a hand on the counter for support. When Jen had come out of prison the first time, she called Anne, her former friend. She had asked Anne if she thought Jen was a fool. Anne decided to be pastoral; she said, only in the way we're called to be fools. Maybe Jen doesn't believe in the calling part anymore; for sure, she feels like a fool. She can't stop the tears.

Then heavy arms come around her from behind, despite the stringent rules about touching one another, and a head is laid against hers. A soft mouth brushes her ear. "Hey girl," Betsy says, "Don't worry about it. Everybody cries in here. There's a lot of shoulders — so many shoulders you wouldn't believe it."

The Child's Position

I am lying on the wet driveway of the military base, in front of the gate barricaded by a couple of dozen military policemen. Actually, I am just inside the gate because I rolled under it. It's April, raining off and on, and cold. I can't get up because a policeman's hand is on my neck. My legs are folded under me in a half-crouch: it is more or less the yoga "child's position," my forehead honoring the earth and incidentally picking up pieces of grit and grass.

Pieces of the gravel are making dents in my palm, but it doesn't hurt if I don't shift my weight. In fact, I can't shift my weight because the policeman's hand becomes heavier when I move.

I hear the women but I can't tell if they are all back outside the gate. I can't see much besides wet blacktop, boots, and trouser legs. Navy and khaki forests of legs restrict my vision. The women are shouting, Let her up. I already asked him that. Maybe I should demand my rights. How do you demand something from this position?

You're hurting her — several voices take it up. I want to shake my head, no, but that's impossible. He's not hurting me, it's just that I can't move, can't see how to proceed. The rain makes it difficult to see much, anyway. My glasses are like a train window in the rain, everything moving by, shimmering.

Am I the only one inside the gate? Did anyone get by the guards? I doubt it. There would be more noise, shouting or chasing. We expected them to stop us. We decided to keep walking toward the commander's office until they stopped us.

I am going to stay here, quiet, unmoving but not submissive, certainly not that, until the strength of my will prevails. I'm a rock, people have said so, I can do it, not be moved . . . and then what?

I wish he could feel my anger pulsing through the back of my neck and it would scorch his hand — or shouldn't I be angry? I can feel my blood in my forehead and below my eyes, behind my eyes, too. I've never seen an angry or embarrassed woman who could blush prettily, delicately. It doesn't happen. When the blood comes, the face tenses and engorges.

Like the policeman who threw me down a few minutes ago, before they slammed the gate: his skin looked swollen and ripe to bursting. I was afraid for him; I thought, a driven personality, probably type A, probably a heavy drinker, to relax. He didn't want to be here, out in the rain; it's probably not his regular duty. He couldn't control his temper when I walked back to the gate and crawled under it. He's probably angry at his own confusion, faced with a dozen singing, capering women who cling to the fence and sing insults at him.

No, we don't do that, that wouldn't be nonviolence, but maybe they perceive our chants as insults; wouldn't I, if someone sang, "nuclear bombs kill housewives, too, doodah, doodah . . . " at me, wouldn't I, peace-loving mom, loving the peace in the evening in my house, a child to smile at, a book, a glass of wine, maybe, wouldn't I be insulted at the suggestion that I was somehow personally responsible for impending devastation? It is an insult.

But his face . . . it's hard to see faces do that, close up, a face that doesn't even know you.

I was seven years old, and Mr. Bruah wanted to hurt me. He didn't even know that the parade was my idea. He had me by the arm and made me drop my sign. I could see the letters LT and NOT KILL sticking out from under his feet. I was proud of that sign — I printed NOT in red and KILL in black and put some fancy curls on the letters so they looked ancient. But they hardly even looked at the letters, they just got angry and started yelling at me and Mr. Bruah grabbed me. He pulled me close to his face so I could see he wasn't kidding. He had his hand on his belt buckle.

Sharon. Remember? how they came from the parted place of birth
. . . the mother almost stands, straining to release the tiny fisted
body, its head pared down to its bone form, the fur slick as an
underwater log, dark, funky, and rich . . . four kittens finally, ears
pasted to their heads in the transparent milky sac, trapping eyes
still shut, beginnings of whiskers, mouths, soundless, opening

"Look, she's gonna have another one."
   "Shh, we have to be quiet."
   "She don't care."
   "Look."
   "That guy can't stand up, where's he going?"
   "Look at their little legs."
   My friend Sharon Bruah's house was next to a vacant lot behind
the neighborhood grocery store, near our school. Mr. Bruah was
always griping about the candy wrappers kids would throw down;
we spent hours picking up candy wrappers and stuffing them into
the barbeque burner he had built. We didn't mind; it gave us an
excuse to rummage in the empty lot next to the store, where we'd
collect pop bottles, two cents apiece. The lot had weeds over our
heads that summer of 1946, and it was good to be out of sight.
   Many of my girlfriends had fathers who were home from the
army, like Mr. Bruah, and the girls said they were glad. More money
made its appearance in the families. But it seemed there was more
hollering, too. Of course, some of that was the new babies, holler-
ing by them and about them. As far as we could see, the best
thing about the babies was that the grownups left us to ourselves
more.
   The day the kittens were born, the grownups were getting ready
for a fourth of July barbeque in Sharon's back yard. We were best
off staying out of the way, Sharon's mom said. So we went to our
hideout under the front porch, and Cat, that's all they called her,
followed us under, meowing like crazy. I guess she needed com-
pany to help her, but we didn't figure out for a long time what
she was doing, crouching and meowing, then coming to us for
petting. We knew she was pregnant all right; she was fat underneath
and all that extra swayed when she ran, slowing her down.

like a woman who's gone into her garden without a sack, and finding ripe tomatoes, lifts up the hem of her blouse to make a pouch, careful so as not to bruise them — not to save the trouble of a sack but for the joy of carrying fruit close to her body

Women are close to the earth. Yes. In this instance, it's certainly true; I couldn't be closer unless I had a shovel. Why am I here? It wasn't that someone came to say, woman, get out of your garden, get off your rear, we need you out at the military base to stop the bomb — they're testing nuclear missiles in war games and you shouldn't let them. Nobody said that in so many words. At first it was curiosity that brought me to a meeting, nothing noble.

I'm not a noble person. I've become too tired for causes; I see where they lead. I have this mental picture of intense long-haired girls of the sixties who sat in meetings and smoked and made proposals and drafted petitions and eventually went away. I was one.

The girls disappear — into marriages, jobs. And the marriages and the children and the jobs are causes, certainly causes, engaging us fully. And what's wrong with that? I'm a rock — maybe in a small river, but a rock — my family, my children run by, lapping and encircling me, I guide the current, they run by. Jobs, tasks also move by and do not move me.

No, not a rock. I'm alive and hurting in this place, held by the scruff of my neck like a kitten.

So they must have been, the small ones, barely dry from their mother's tongue and the water again claimed them, filled quickly their nostrils and throats — surprised by death as a few minutes before surprised by life. Curious, to wonder which was least painful.

"Sharon, where were you? Why weren't you marching with me?"

Sharon pointed to Marianne. "Twerp here, this stupid little *brat*, locked the door!"

"I'm going to *tell!*" Marianne screwed up her face trying to screw out tears.

"Go ahead, tell, crybaby, bitchbaby!" Sharon really was crying, her face dark as a winesap apple, her freckles darker. She hated her sister, had always hated her, her milkeyed bedmate, smaller and holier always. Marianne was hardly ever in trouble, and if she was, she found a way to blame someone. "Sharon wanted me to," she'd say with her pale eyes widening as though she believed it and could see nothing wrong with following her sister.

And I followed Sharon too, like the time we sneaked into the wrong line during air raid drill and mixed up the teacher's count. Then we sneaked back. The teacher never did figure out if anyone was missing. This time, though, it was my idea and I was first.

It was Cindy, Marianne's dumb girlfriend, who told us. She came inside where we were coloring to get out of the way of the barbeque and she told us Mr. Bruah had drowned the kittens. I don't know how Cindy found out, but it was true. Sharon's mother was at the sink. She just nodded without looking at us and filled glasses with ice and left us.

I was the one who had the idea about the signs. I thought we could show Mr. Bruah and the grownups that they were wrong to do what they did. We couldn't exactly argue with them, it was too late anyway, but we could make a parade like on Memorial Day. We'd have signs. Marianne was the neatest letterer in first grade. Everybody was proud of her. And I was the best speller.

I never wanted to be a leader, that is, to go first. I'm not sure why that is—I tend to think something will go wrong, like I'll forget the date or someone's name, or be late, and the program will fail. Just give me a job, I say, tell me what to do. Or let me watch a while. I didn't even want to come today. I think I finally came because I was tired of being undecided. I was tired of seeing these women link arms, it seemed, unconsciously; I would have liked such instinctive knowing.

My present position, now, is fairly clear: a man, about 175 pounds I'd say, has a portion of his weight on top of me. Pale yellow grass is sticking to his left boot, a few inches from my nose. A half-drowned worm has its head, I suppose it's the head, swaying cobra-style awfully close to my left hand. This is the time of worms— not as many as after midsummer rains, just a few slow pink, gray-belted ones have fled the soaked earth and are taking their chances on asphalt. Julie said she saw an MP crush one.

Julie — hardly older than my own children — said once that when she was growing up she thought maybe it was a good thing the bomb would kill so many people, that the earth would be cleaner. But then she realized the animals would be gone, too.

We were ready. Everyone had a sign. Marianne had a picture of a cat on hers but it was the kind of cat like a snowman, one ball with ears, on top of a bigger ball with a curvy line for a tail. It didn't look anything like the kittens.

When I opened the back door to go into the yard, the sun hit me, and I couldn't see really well. I couldn't look at the grownups, anyway. I just marched staring straight ahead. I knew that it was serious business. I tried to keep from smiling, but I could feel my smile muscles trying to work, because I was embarrassed. I was just going to march around once, in a circle.

Our plan was to blockade as long as possible. A good deal of discussion was spent on how long we could stay. None of us is prepared to say we have nothing better to do. Measuring nuclear madness against our jobs, appointments, mealtimes, children, lovers' preferences is difficult, when the terms are one military gate in a midwestern city in an April drizzle that is widening into stilettos of sleet.

Between the fingers on my neck I can feel the rain sharpen, and the hand shifts; it shifts water, releasing a runnel that slides under my shirt and around to the front of me. The next trickle will be colder. I want to shrug deeper into my poncho to protect my bare neck, which is wearing only a hand, but the hand tightens again. A second runnel seeks new territory, but joins the first. My breasts are sticking to my brassiere. The feeling is familiar, and comforting.

With my second baby I had to carry handkerchiefs; the milk would leap up whether the baby was there or not. We, breast and baby, tried to arrange the feeding so that I could work in an office. He'd have bottles while I worked and he'd nurse morning, evening, and night times. Coffee break was fifteen minutes on a breast pump, crying half the time because I couldn't make it work and the damn milk would come a half hour later at someone's soft word or the leaves moving outside the office window. Six months like that, milk looking for babies and running joyous just before quitting time, the clock watcher leaning toward home and feeding time. I remember that time John Stenson, Patti's husband, caught me in the office cramming a washcloth inside my blouse . . . his arms trapped mine and in the window reflection I saw his eyes, tender and not surprised, just let me look, he said, how lovely, I just want to look, but his hand was sliding over milk.

This grip today, not sexual, not after these long minutes, both of us held in this situation . . . he's afraid. Of what? That I'll shame him in front of his company. He looks powerful only while he's holding me. When he lets go, what?

Maybe I'll remember the principles of martial arts, to use the strength of your attacker. To find it, I'll push at the ground with my hands, humping my back and then let go just before his hands push back. He'd fall on me then, but my poncho is slippery and furthermore becomes tangled in his arms and the cheap plastic snaps pull loose. For a second, the wet plastic hood is over my face, there is darkness, and blood beats behind my eyes, the smell of blood in my nostrils . . . then I'm free, off and running, I find the right building, stride through the office doors past three workers, women trim in blue uniforms with skirts. The commander is present, not out of the city as we've been told, and I plunk down the water-soaked press statement, limp and dripping, but readable. He frowns at it a moment, reading, adjusting his wire-rimmed glasses on an authoritative but not belligerent nose, then looks at me directly with truth in his eyes, and we stop the war games.

What really happens is that I struggle to get up and am caught in my poncho. The MP pushes me back, scooting me on my stomach, back underneath the gate. The women help me up, I am stiff and weepy for a few minutes, they encircle me in their arms. A few of us talk, back and forth, with the soldiers behind the gate. Julie argues with a reporter who wants to emphasize the futility of small acts like ours. After a short time, a soldier brings a thermos of coffee, and some of the men share it with us. One soldier comments that if you treat protestors like human beings you can usually avoid trouble.   •

When Mr. Bruah let go of my arm, there were no children but me in the back yard. I had been a parade all by myself. The grownups yelled at me, but I didn't stop to listen. The words left trails somewhere, though, and I understood that I could not have been right about my signs. They said I didn't have any right; who did I think I was? When I crept back into the house, Sharon and Marianne were arguing whose fault it was that they didn't join me outside. Cindy went home. After a while, I went home too.

But I don't believe him this time. Maybe I didn't believe him then. I kept thinking: But I saw them. I saw the kittens being born. I know better than him. I will not be reasonable, I am a child, I am a woman with children. There will be trouble and I will be part of it.

The Violators

Nance, I want to tell you that I've spent seventy-five days in jail, eight short sentences for protesting bombs and killing. I tell people that I don't remember the numbers, and I have to take out paper and pencil to figure out the times. But I do remember. That is, I remember each day, singly. And I remember the women in jail, their ages and colors — mostly young, mostly African-American, and their "crimes," mostly keeping their men, the pimps and the pushers, on the outside. These are violated women. For me jail isn't that hard. It isn't jail where I feel violated.

Maybe there was no real beginning. I do know there are times now when a part of me wakes and snarls that for years has been schooled into acceptance. The chief was present during one awakening. I wanted to tell you then, but it was too soon; then the time was telescoped for you. The time was never right.

We went together to see the chief because we couldn't go home. We'd been together the night before, you remember, at the Sisters of Saint Joseph's house, most of us on the living room floor. We'd been together on laps or under hips in the big Olds on the rainy way to Honeywell. You pulled off to the shoulder on 35W to unload the rest of us, handing us the rug. I knew you desperately wanted to come. You stayed long enough to see us climb the embankment. We slipped over the freeway fence with some difficulty, first throwing the rug over the barbs on top, helping each other over as we'd rehearsed. Some of the blood caked on my shin was from that.

I thought the chief had authority. We'd be justified, our emotional wounds eased; he was, after all, on "our" side. He'd be assiduous in directing arrests, but he understood the larger issues. He'd be upright, a stern peacekeeper but a moral one. I believed he had class.

What I meant by class wasn't that the chief was upper middle, or monied, or that he'd risen to a position — vital as an ailanthus tree springing up in a sidewalk grating — I meant urbane and ready-tongued. The chief was at home in his world. He'd give the same ear to Myra, the wing-haired bag lady who hung out in the downtown library, as to a councilman with a hot issue. He was quick, he'd fill in the words that they forgot in their ravings.

I thought I knew something about class issues. After all, twenty-five years ago, I married above my class. I was tardy in seeing that I had done so: I loved, I was a new convert to their Texas Democratic politics, which I confused with democratic principles. The remarks of my mother-in-law came too obliquely. They were insidious, but they did cut, slowly, through my fog of romanticism and rectitude.

She said, "My son will help you form taste in these matters." She said (to my husband), "She does not know which fork to use" (the topic was not forks but my hesitancy in social contexts). She said, "You and he have grown up in different worlds." (I thought, one world.) She said, "He has had many advantages." (I used my broadest South Chicago nasal "Yeah, so?" but to myself.) My sense of injury was partly offset by my assurance that she hadn't come into the modern age; she didn't know any better. My gentle resistance to her barbs, I thought, would help her mature into truer human relations. I've had some problems with moral arrogance.

Would you shake your head? You never liked self-deprecatory statements, even when I was trying to be funny. You said, don't give your power away.

See, it's about power. The first Thanksgiving he and I spent with his family, my husband would redden when his mother rang a little silver bell. This was for Lily in the kitchen, a signal to clear the plates and bring coffee and dessert. The kitchen wasn't that far away, only the other side of a swinging door. "Mother, must you?"

"Well, of course I don't when only the two of us are dining. But Lily prefers it." I think the argument was that when we "children" were visiting, Lily had more work to do and needed a signal to stop doing one thing and start doing another.

My husband never went so far as to suggest that Lily eat supper with us. But he was chided for talking about civil rights at the table.

In that house in 1964, such conversation went beyond the bounds of good taste, even assuming the bell ritual would keep the help out of earshot. And after the first time I tried to clear the plates, and was told gently by my father-in-law to sit down, Lily would do it, I didn't offer again. I suppose those were some of the first soft prods of oppressions against my thick-skinned soul. I identified with Lily, but I don't think she identified with me.

What does all this have to do with you, Nance, or the chief? You remember, you asked me, "What is your class background?" on one of the few occasions we were alone, without the group. You'd brought smoked country ham from your grandpa's farm in MissouRAH (you insisted), a dark creamy horseradish, and near-black pumpernickel in slabs. Sitting on the rug in front of my tape deck, we listened to ourselves on the radio telling the story of our first time in jail. Between mouthfuls, we laughed and hugged each other in delight at our brilliance.

You were beautiful then, Nance. We had teen-aged sons the same age, but you wore your skin stretched tight over your freckles and delicate facial bones. You had the looks and energy of a woman ten years younger. I knew you'd been out as a lesbian for years, and were a Wiccan guide; to me, you shone with passion and spiritual strength.

I wasn't sure what you were asking me about class. "Middle," I supposed, not rich, not poor; my family owned our mortgage in South Chicago. My dad had gone to college and worked at Bethlehem Steel, then at Hines Lumber. My mother worked part-time as a clerk in a drug store, and I took casseroles out of the oven and ironed my brothers' shirts. I went to college, too; my brothers didn't but made good money. "Mixed," you said. "Mixed up," I responded and told you about my husband's family. "So what are you?" I challenged.

"Oh, working class. My family doesn't get what we're doing."

I nodded. Families. I knew your son lived out of state, on the farm with grandparents, but I thought it was a matter of supporting him. Your tax resistance meant you kept free of seizeable assets; for a single working woman in the 1980s, staying poor was certainly possible, but your road was a harsher one than any I could imagine for myself. Still, I thought I'd come some way politically since 1964 and I wasn't willing to be identified with the ruling class.

So; back to the chief. You refused to go over the fence with us — remember? You'd drive, then you'd go back to the gates that Honeywell erected at the main entrance, to be part of the swell of supporters. "I can't do it this time," you said, "maybe not again." You, Nance, who ordinarily would lead an action for the physical joy of leaping the fence, or of singing in a circle covered with ponchos against the drizzle, a communal umbrella.

"I have some issues to work out." Your problem, I gathered, was with the police, who as was customary in large demonstrations had been notified. You were against negotiating the means of arrest with police. "They're our enemies," you declared, rubbing your wrists.

The argument was familiar to me: police are tools of the state, they can't help it, they're trained to violence and repression. The picture didn't fit with plump Jimmy Bald, my brothers' childhood buddy, or with Chuck of my journaling group, who trembled when he told the story of a jumper he'd tried to reach, and missed.

"They're human beings," I insisted, "individuals." In our non-violence training at the Women's Peace Camp, we practiced ways to talk to the authorities. The peace camp at Sperry Defense Systems in St. Paul had lasted a year, through the thirty-inch snows and thirty-below nights of 1983–84, the year of the Euromissiles. We discussed practical pleas, "Don't hurt us, we're just going to sit down here," and impractical, "you don't have to arrest us."

"I know," you said, "you talk to them. And what do they say to you?" I thought maybe you were angry because you'd been tightly handcuffed at a sit-in a few days before. You went on, "One guy said to me, 'We have trouble with lesbians.'"

"He could have meant, he didn't understand . . . " I began, then didn't know how to finish. I looked into your eyes laughing at me, until one spilled over. You didn't cry any more than that. You said, "He put the cuffs on while we were sitting down — he said to stay down. Then he said, get up, and we couldn't move fast so he jerked me up by my wrists. You know how that hurts?" I didn't. "The police don't like us," you said.

I thought you were exaggerating. "Listen," I said, "we can't pretend we're in a revolutionary struggle. We're not an oppressed people. We have to accept these laws, our police. Isn't it part of taking the consequences to . . . ?"

You laid your hand on my arm. "I'm not talking about *you,* I'm talking about *us.*" It was my turn to cry.

You'd think I'd have had warning enough by that wet morning.

Early that morning, having practiced twice in the sisters' back yard, peace commandos, we six had set up our symbolic tent in two minutes flat. The banner we'd decorated during the long night with suns and animals and woman-signs snapped in the gusts of April sleet like laundry on the line. We were going to be welcomers to the hundreds of predawn protestors coming with their ladders for the action. We would claim the Honeywell park for our new women's camp, proclaim peace at the doors of the bombmakers.

You know what happened next. You were still outside the gate, but I kept asking myself, what would Nance do?

We took down our tent after an hour or so of picketing, then met in a circle to decide what to do when arrests began. Mim declared she wasn't going to line up to be arrested. The police hadn't given us the traditional warning, since we'd gone in from the freeway, not over the front gate with the orderly lines of police waiting below. We peacefully picnicked on the lawn while the police numbered off those clambering over the ladders. Most of the group thought maybe we should just leave and go to breakfast. By the time my turn in the circle came, my moral fibers were itching; I said we couldn't have our fun, then leave everyone else to go through the courts.

How might we continue resisting, in a peaceful way? Mary spotted the traffic cones, stacked inside the gate in case 28th Street needed rerouting during the protest. We lifted several of them, plunked them in a neat line in the middle of Honeywell's driveway, and sat down. The first police vanload of protestors was moving from the front door, and the gates were just opening to allow the vans through. We were in the way.

In the police wagon, some of us cried — but not for lack of spirit, only from the immediate pain. I remember trying to work in as many words as possible while the police lifted and heaved. It was a moment of adrenalin and desperation, like scrubbing your house the night before surgery, a talismatic action to forestall a slip of the knife. Say why I am here before the doors clang shut. "Honeywell's in Lebanon, South Africa! Honeywell makes cluster bombs, Honeywell weapons are in El Salvador, bombing campesinos, mothers, babies!" I said Libya too, although we didn't know that for sure. Someone laughed at the rush of words.

Our hands were bound behind us, so that it was difficult to roll to a sitting position; but we had to roll, to keep from being stacked like human cordwood as the men threw us in. You must have been handcuffed like that, too — with the plastic strap that is looped around your wrists and threaded through a catch that slides only one way. If you try to work it loose, the strap tightens, and you can't change your mind and loosen it again. It hurts. They have to cut it off later, much later.

Robert, of the Friends, who was well dressed in a suit and must have looked like Honeywell security, came running to take pictures. That's how we happened to have evidence of the policeman kneeling over a woman's rear end, grimacing with the effort of yanking the cuffs tight.

I could hear you yelling at the chief, some time after Robert's pictures and before the van took off. "There are women hurting in there, chief, chief damn you, look at them!" Robert must have gone to the gate to report. I heard later he'd told the protestors inside the grounds, at the front door, but no one else came to witness or to help. I suppose the police would have stopped them. I wonder about it sometimes.

Did you know how I admired your voice? It was so strong, a clear contralto that aimed itself. When you sang with a quartet your voice blended with the rest, but even in a crowded auditorium I would hear your voice as though your song were coming straight to me.

You were behind the "keening" demonstrations. You'd lift your throat to the high ceilings of government offices, bringing home to the officials the dead and our sorrow. We women would close our eyes to go within ourselves and remember the voices of women and children from Central America, our visitors from Leon, Nicaragua — Ruth, Maria, Brenda; or America Sosa; or Terese from Sanctuary. Or we'd pull a moan of shame over "our" war from behind our breastbones, letting it rise and gather courage in concert. I was never particularly good at it, busy watching the color fade from the officials before they'd leave the room. Even our own men paled; some of them parted their lips, but no sound came, and you could tell they wanted it to be over.

I miss the song *and* the shouting. Most of the keening was wordless, but one time I remember especially, you went to my heart, wailing "You can't have my son, you can't have my baby!" "They" already had him, you explained later; he was waiting only until he was of age, wild to join the army.

The point is, there was no way the chief could not have heard your voice. But the doors clanged shut and that bruising ride began.

Afterward, we expected to file a complaint, but a crisp-bloused officer who I concluded was the gatekeeper, declared, "You can't do that." She said, "You can't go inside in a bunch, people are swayed by each other's statements; maybe someone experienced the event in a different way and that person would be unduly influenced by the others." "Right," we said, "we just want to talk to the chief." So she told us to call for an appointment, one at a time, maybe next week. We talked awhile longer, then walked out and down the hall, until we saw the chief's name on another door. We walked in.

He was pacing up and down his outer office, where the desk was empty of its keeper, and he was looking at the floor. He glanced up, scowling at the sudden appearance of these various ladies (they call you "lady" often at police stations, as a term of address). The chief had an expressive forehead, tall and full-browed; his eyebrows alone could do half the work of a glare. He walked us into his office, and waved at the chairs around the room. We pulled them to a semicircle, the best we six could do to surround a big desk for a big man.

At least the desk was not nude, swept clean to fit the recommendations of corporate advisors. The chief's desk was piled with reports, forms and folders, three-ring binders, and newspaper articles. A cup filled with pens tipped against a standard phone with lighted buttons. He looked busy enough, but apparently other people wrote and reported to keep his desk at an appropriate level of untidiness; he'd stay on top of things. A midsize window overlooked Third Avenue; it was high enough that a building corner and a small piece of sky to the west was all the view.

The day had cleared. In a couple of hours, the chief's window would have a share in that calm time of uniform indigo, when sky and snow and the glass facades of newer buildings would be the same color. I lean toward that color and wait for it. Blemishes dissolve, and the evening light infuses the city snow with an intensity that is neither day nor night, but a promise. It doesn't last long. I wondered if the chief used his window, if he had time for reflection. Now, of course, the light was harsher, the sun glinting off something metallic on the building opposite. I suddenly remembered the gatekeeper had worn a gun. I couldn't tell if, underneath his suit coat, the chief had his.

We'd been inside being processed all day since the wagon, and I was woolgathering; I didn't hear his first words. Apparently he would listen to us in turn, beginning at the right end of our row of chairs, who was Alison. Alison was pale, but she has that sort of complexion that invests all the color in her lips. Normally they are full and mobile; you can't help watching her slow smile. Today they were stiff with indignation. She was fifteen, my youngest son's age. "Two of them *threw* me in, on my belly. And after I got up and looked at them they grinned at me and made kissing noises, like this." She showed how they did it, then she turned away and gagged. The chief didn't see or hear the gagging, apparently. He nodded to Marge to be next.

Marge lived with the sisters then, and was considering a religious vocation. I could see she was determined to be fair. The weal on her cheek wouldn't purple into a bruise for a few more hours but it was already obvious. "Maybe they didn't mean to hit my face against the floor. What was intentional was strapping the cuffs so tight, and . . . "

Mim jumped in, "They said, that's the last time you'll ever put your hands out in front of you!" The chief ignored her except for a 'wait your turn' twitch of his head.

"They jerked our hands to the back," Marge continued, firmly making Mim's point, "We couldn't balance ourselves for that crazy driving, we were on the floor and we couldn't hold on to the benches — they did it on purpose, didn't they? To throw us around in the van?"

"Show me your wrists," the chief said, quietly enough. He nodded his head several times, making it clear he looked at everyone's hands front and back. Mary's and mine were the ugliest. The police had had a hard time cutting her cuffs off, they were so deeply embedded. Our wrists showed a double indented track with a few square red pits between them. An inch or so on the outside of the tracks was a thin line of congealed blood where the plastic had cut the skin. He seemed to forget about taking turns, because he started to make a speech.

"So this is about the sum of it, the wrists, the fast driving. . . ."

"Not just fast," Mary interrupted, "crazy! He slammed on the brakes, stopped and started a dozen times to jerk us around. . . ." The chief flinched at the phrase and stared at her. "There are several lights between Honeywell and downtown. He had instructions to proceed with due speed."

I was beginning to be confused. "You were at Honeywell. You must have seen him start, seen the way they . . . " Remember, Nance? He was a few feet from the van, in a long dark trench coat and narrow-brimmed hat pulled low against the sleet, but not against watching. There was no doubt in my mind that he was watching everything.

"Please," he went on, "I respect your position, but I don't — and I've told your leaders this and maybe some of you," he looked around but there was no recognition in his eyes that I could see — "I don't agree with your methods." Alison began to say something, but his words swallowed hers. "I want you to hear me. I want us to hear each other." He was the only one talking now. "I just want you to look in your hearts. You say violence was done to you. I want you to think about whether you were provocative."

It seemed an odd word to me, from a man who was intentional in his use of descriptive words. Provocative is what they say of women who entice. Provocative blouses are lacy, see-through . . . "My client, your honor, believed the woman was provocative, that she desired it. . . ." The other day, Nance, a friend told me a story about the chief. He said, once the chief was in an elevator with my girlfriend. She's standing in front of him. She doesn't know him, they're strangers, but she knows who he is. All of a sudden, the chief turns to a guy next to him and says quietly, coolly, but you know his voice has an edge that slides through ambient sound and bounces off corners — he says, "This woman behind me has her hands all over my body." He says this just before the doors open and he saunters out.

Yes, it was a story — but it fit the popular impression of the chief, doing the unexpected, but in control. You know how I felt, Nance? When my friend told me the story he was laughing, but I couldn't even smile after all that time. Years ago, before I knew you, I might have smiled. I'd seen the chief at fundraisers, chuckling over a spoof of the police, or stooping to catch the words of elderly activists.

One thing more about that morning before we saw the chief. When we arrived downtown and the doors opened, a smiling policeman was there to help us out. Except that he didn't extend his hand, just said watch it. Our hands being still bound, the process involved inching and sliding to the doors on our backsides and finding handholds behind us as we jumped down. Not graceful. I nodded at the policeman, expecting — what? Acknowledgment of a common predicament, caught at the same moment, part of the same event, of cosmic ridicule. He said, "What was all that crying back there? You dykes sound like a bunch of fucking goats!"

The chief acknowledged that the experience must have been unpleasant for us. "But I can say, while I admit I didn't see everything, I saw no indication of violence. The officers acted appropriately to the situation."

"Appropriate!" someone, not me, objected, "How were the ways they hurt us appropriate?"

"In my years in New York and here," the chief continued, "police brutality is a fact we have to contend with, but this on the face of it was not violence."

My head cleared at his words. Of course; it was a matter of degree. Alison hadn't been beat up by the wiseacre cop, with his smacking lips; she wasn't hurt except in ways that didn't matter to the chief or to the police. Our cuts and bruises would heal. I wanted to clarify his words; I said, "Then you're saying violence is something else. Throwing us down isn't violence, or making sure the cuffs are painful, or driving to bang us around, trying to hurt us just enough . . . "

He didn't wait for the rest of my fumbling words, whatever they might have been. I felt as though I was exploring some new and rough terrain, like wet, saw-toothed grasses, with inadequate protection. I was moving too slowly. The chief slapped his hand on the desk and his face turned dark, pure cop: "You do not define violence for me, madam! I define violence for myself!"

I guess this is by way of apology to you, Nance, that I have been moving so slowly. I had to experience it in my own skin before

I understood how you had been hurt. And in that same moment I knew myself a violator; in that dark face I saw another one — the cop who called me a name I couldn't accept. Somewhere in the rush of anger that followed the chief's words, I recognized a rageful child who wanted to declare my "straightness," just to prove them wrong, about something. Forget about solidarity, or love.

I never told you about that experience; you might have appreciated it. Sometimes when I want to comfort myself for not being one of the sisters you gathered around your dying, I imagine taking you in my arms to tell you stories like this one.

Carol Masters grew up in Chicago during the 1940s and 1950s in two South Side neighborhoods. As a student, graduate student, and faculty wife she lived in Bloomington, IL, Manhattan, KS, Vermillion, SD, and Kingsville, TX. In the early 1980s, Masters's children and their friends got her involved in the anti-nuclear movement. She has since spent time in jail for nonviolent protests at weapons contractors' doors and senators' offices.

Through the last decade, Masters has volunteered and worked as staff in several social change organizations, including the Minnesota Peace and Justice Coalition, Women Against Military Madness, and the Honeywell Project. She currently works for Habitat for Humanity, and lives in Minneapolis with her second husband.